THICK AS THIEVES

Billie Dureya Shell

THICK AS THIEVES

Copyright © 2021

All rights reserved to Billie Dureyea Shell.

No part of this publication may be reproduced, distributed or transmitted in any form or by any means, including photocopying, or other electronic or mechanical methods, without the prior written permission of the publisher, except in the case of brief quotations embodied in critical reviews and certain noncommercial uses permitted by copyright law.
Any references to historical events, real people or real places are used factiously. Names, characters, and places are products of the authors imagination.

Front Cover Image By grafic designer Billie Dureyea Shell & Kenny Writes

First Printing Edition 2021

ISBN 978-2-7350234-9-6

This Book Is Dedicated

To My Son Dillion I love you and I always got

your back NO MATTER WHAT

ACKNOWLEDGEMENT

First and foremost I have to give honor to My Lord And Saviour Jesus Christ without him now of this would be possible. 2020 was a MUTHA FUCCA Corona Virus made shit hard 4 niggas but we made it threw y'all keep your head up and know that God got us, no matter they throw in our way no one can stop what God has plan for you...
Its 2021 now FUCC 2020 and Covid 19.... Now to my family momma I love you and you no I got you no matter what. You mean the world 2 me oh and NO MORE PINCHING LOL. To my little sister Glenda I love you blackie, you No I Got You always

To my Wife Shatoya Shell you get on my damn nerves 👧 but I wouldnt trade you 4 anything In the world I love ♥ you more then words can ever express. To all my children 👭 I love y'all Jazmine, Ant'Tuan, Davon, Anthony, David, Lil Dureyea, Alura, Queen Diavion, Cameron, Preniece, Shaniece and Tajh I love u all and I'll 4ever have ur back you all give me a reason 2 smile... to my cousin Zane RIP nigga I miss u more then anyone will ever no, your always remembered love you bro. to my cousin Ty I miss you thank 4 looking out 4 me and Zane you played a big part in my life and I always looked up to you I love you... Uncle Woody I miss you and love you, you no your my favorite uncle... To my nigga Jamal love you, my brothers Lawrence and fred thank 4 showing me the game I love yall 4 that. To my oldest sister Nedra love you thank you 4 always having my back. to my family uncles anties cousins etc.. I love y'all even those of you that act funny as fuck

To my dark side niggas y'all no what it is YAAH GANG....
Now to all my readers and fans I love you thanks for reading I
hope u enjoy this book as much as I enjoy writing
them with this Corona Virus 19 shit there ain't shit to do but
write so I'm on my shit with that being said y'all be safe cover
your face and love each other life is short so love the ones that
really love I'm gone no. enjoy the book

STAY SAFE

Author Billie Dureyea Shell

THERE'S NOTHING U CANNOT DO

IF U PUT UR MIND 2 IT.

All you nigga's got EDD money so aint no excuse

why you can't get a book LOL

Chapter One

LITTLE MALCOLM

As I sat on Auntie's Mya's couch, I thought about all the things that I had gone through. When the white man came to get me from Auntie Mya's house when she was keeping us, I did not know if he was on the up and up, but I had to trust it because I wanted to see my Mama. After the hours of driving we finally pulled up to the apartment that looked abandoned. I was scared to death but when I saw my Mother but also, I was happy as hell. I cried tears of joy so when we were separated again it messed with me. When Mama pulled up at Auntie Mya' house I was happy as hell. I did not know what to think or say. I was holding it together, but I have to admit that I was falling apart. First, I had lost my father and then I was thinking I had lost my Mama. I was scared when those niggas came blasting, their guns when we were in that little apartment building. Shit Mama was pacing back and forth and all nervous the entire time we were hiding out. I did not know what was going on, but I knew that the police had us. I did not know what Mama had done but she was always getting locked up like when my brothers' Mama Cedes tried to frame my Mother for the death of her girlfriend who was my Aunt Nessa that was wild. Mama got out of that jam now I wanted to know what was going on? Mama was always caught up in the middle of some shit it was like Trouble was her middle name. Mama had told me that our stepfather Rashad was dead, and it broke my heart. I loved that man. He always treated me right. He took me everywhere with him. I didn't like how he sometimes had women in the car with us. When Mama wasn't in the car but when we hung out it was so much fun. He would always tell me "son don't tell your Mother what we did today. If she asks, let her know we did man things" I would always hold my end of the bargain. Rashad was not like the other guy my mother had dated Bruce. I hated him. Whenever Mama would leave us alone with him, he would say little things like you little nigga babies or bastards. I didn't know what it meant at the time, but I knew I did not like him. The way his eyes would look at us with disgust was harsh. I thought my Mama was never coming back but she did. I liked staying with Auntie Mya and Uncle Tre. Uncle Tre was cool as hell and when I would ride the city with him. He got much love from the dope boys on the streets. You would think with him working so closely with the police that the drug dealers would hate him, but they loved him. We heard a car pull into the driveway and then a door slam. I was in the living room watching cartoons with my little sister she was so cute and fun. She had changed though since that day that we left, and the cop had gotten killed. She was still happy, but she had a difference to her that I could not quite understand. I still loved her though she was all I had. Auntie Mya went to the window and looked out of it. Her face lit up and she ran to the door "Oh my God!" She screamed. I wanted to know what the hell was going on. She opened the door and ran out of it and I went to see what was going on. As I made it to the doorway, I saw the most beautiful face I had ever seen. My heart stopped and I could feel the tears that I had been hiding emerge from my tear duct. I felt the warmness of them slide down my face and a smile crept up on me. "Mama!" I yelled and ran into her arms. She had come back for us.

Little Deena

The day that Mama showed up I was happy. Hell, I missed my Mama but what I wasn't happy about was this new nigga in her life. No, he hadn't harmed me and my brother but shit he was just another nigga that came in my life and would probably leave. I loved my father and when he died a piece of me died with him. I liked Bruce he would always treat me good and buy me things and when he left a piece of me left with him too. When my Mother married Rashad, I was happy. Rashad was a handsome man and he was very generous with his money. He took me on shopping sprees and sometimes he would take me over his sisters' house. I would play with their kids while he went in his sisters' rooms and talked. I especially liked his sister Trickzy she was different with her colorful hair. Her kids were my cousins and I missed them. Rashad always told me never to mention them to Mama because Mama was jealous of Trickzy and I did not see why. Mama had everything that you could ask for a big house, clothes, jewelry, a nice car, a pretty smile and she always kept her hair done. Mama was a bad bitch if you asked me. Trickzy was okay but she was not Mama that was for sure. I loved my Mama and hated her at the same time. She was everything I wanted to be in a woman and everything I didn't want to be. She was strong and loving, smart and loud, her sense of style was amazing for a big girl. But I noticed something about Mama she lacked happiness. She may have loved us, but we didn't make her one hundred percent happy. When I saw her that day after all those months, I was happy to say the least. Maurice was standing there crying and it made me want to cry but I couldn't. Maurice ran into her arms and I just stood there looking at the interaction. I loved Mama but something was missing for her and I wanted to make sure she had it. Once she got done with Maurice she looked around until she found me. Her eyes glistened and she had love in them. I could tell my Mother missed us, but I was a bit mad at her for leaving. For putting us in that situation. When I closed my eyes, I could still see that man's brain splatter all over the wall. I didn't know how Malcolm felt about it but did something to me. I don't know what it was? I was not the same. Nope A' Deena Alana Harris is not the same I am Danity now. Mama came up to me and hugged me and I loved the scent of her perfume. She was going to smother me with her love. I loved the way she hugged me and at first. I was not going to show emotions, but her warmth and love entangled into my heart. I missed my Mama, I loved my Mama, I cherished my Mama, and I really did miss my Mama and I was glad that she was here. The tears fell from my eyes she was everything to me.

I used to be Aniya

The day that I reunited with my kids was the happiest day of my life. I mean damn I could not believe I had been away from them that long! And for what? Huh, this time I was not going to mess anything up. I had already talked with the FEDS and got my name cleared for the killing of Dale. I had to make things right. I needed money most of all. I told them about Jeff and that was all. Crenshaw gave me his Uncle's location and I gave it to the police. I lied and told them that that is where he held me and that is where I escaped. I had to testify and this time I did not give a damn I told on his ass. The cops said that they would help me leave and relocate I declined their offer. I had money and I was going to change my name and sell my businesses and start over, but I did not need their help. I pulled up to the house that I knew was Mya. The cops had helped me locate them and I was happy. They had a nice two-story brick house and I was happy that I had decided to leave my kids with her. Crenshaw's sister was back at the hotel with her kids. I got out the car and Mya came running out to the car crying. She looked crazy as hell all that hair on her head was wild. "I missed you I am so happy you are alive!" She cried. I embraced her and I loved the way she felt. She was a true comfort, a true friend. My little Malcolm was standing in the doorway crying. He looked like his father and when he came to me, I embraced him. He was my little man. It felt good hugging him and I did not want this feeling to end. I looked over to my Deena and she stood in the doorway with a stern look on her face. She was an angel. That round face with that curly hair she was beautiful. I walked up to her and gave her a hug. I felt her loosen up and she cried. We had always had a touchy relationship, but I knew that she loved me at that very moment and I damn sure loved her.

My new life Crenshaw

The look that Niya had when she saw her kids was priceless. I had to admit I loved that woman. Yes, she had made me turn against my family but when family is not doing right then sometimes you have to pick your own road. I was happy that I had gotten my sister and her kids out of there before they ever figured anything out because if I lost them then I would be heartbroken. I waited for the reunion to come to an end. Niya came back to the car and grabbed my hand. She led me in the house. Her friend had a beautiful house and her friend was beautiful. Her long curly hair was exotic, and she had the sexiest face I had ever seen. I mean Niya was beautiful, but her friend was gorgeous. We sat down and they talked with each other. I had bought the kids some toys so that they could play. I had gotten her son an Xbox One and her daughter I bought her a bike. I did not know what they had and didn't have so I just picked out simple things. I went in the room with her son and when we got in the room, he hugged me. "Thanks for saving us" he said with tears. At first, I didn't know what to say. He had made me feel some type of way. "Aw it wasn't nothing lil man" I said, and we hooked up his game. We were silent as we played the Xbox. I had told him that it wasn't nothing, but it was huge. What I had done for them altered my life and I did not know if that was good or bad.

I am in disbelief Mya

I could not believe she was back. I shot Tre a text while Niya was in the living room talking to Danity. I had not told her the name changes that they had made yet. I just knew that I wanted everything to go back to normal for these kid's sake. She looked good too. Her short hair was dyed red and spiked up. She had lost a significant amount of weight, but she still had her hips on her and most importantly she looked happy. This guy that was with her was a thug I could tell. He looked way too young to be a special friend of hers but the way she looked at him you could tell that he was. I had enjoyed the kids, but I was happy that their mother was home. She came in the kitchen where I was drinking a glass of milk. "We need to talk Mya," I was happy that she said it. She sat in a chair across from me. "Mya thanks for everything I mean it. It is time for us to leave I just came to get the kids. I had to testify against a very dangerous man, and I have to take the kids, my money, and sell my businesses." I couldn't believe that she had walked in here ready to snatch her companies from underneath me when I had made them so much money. "Your businesses I have been making the money for you since you have been playing Jane Bonds and shit." I told her. I didn't mean to come off so harsh, but she had lost her mind. She looked at me a bit hurt. "You don't know what I have been through so don't you dare say shit to me. You didn't have to do shit that was your choice I need to sell that shit to keep my kids safe!" She yelled. I could tell she was more hurt than angry. I was wrong I did not know why I was tripping hell I really did not have to work. "You are right, and I am sorry." I just wanted all this bullshit to be over. I got up and was heading out the kitchen. "Wait Mya you should come with us." She said.

I am not who they think I am Tre

Mya texted me to tell me that Niya was back. I really did not give a fuck. Just when I had planned on moving us this bitch come back into the picture. Huh she was getting on my nerves. She kept showing up and disappearing. I knew her and that nigga Rashad was into some deep shit. I had tried to reach out to her, but she never called me. Man, they were not making any money but if they fucked with me then they would have come up. Montre Kahlee Williams was my name and I am the muthafucking man! Yes, I work with the police shit so I can know who the bosses and bossettes were so that I could do business with them. Private Invest igat or yeah, I privately investigated these fuck niggas and put a bullet through they head. I was a multimillionaire and my wife Mya had no idea. I did not know how to tell her that her husband was the muthafucking man! I had sold everything out here on these streets just like Mitch in Paid in Full I loved the hustle. I had branched off now and was doing hits for the police. Hell, yeah them muthafuckas was dirty too but a nigga like me loved it. I pulled up to the house two hours after getting her text. I was not very happy about coming home but I had to play the part. I walked into the house and saw Danity sitting on the couch. I don't know what it was about that little girl but when she came back this second time, she was different. Not in a bad way but in a good way that I liked. "What up niecey Pooh what are you watching?" "Nothing really" she said flicking through channels. I walked in the kitchen and looked at the two women before me. Niya was gorgeous just like I remembered. It was something about her that made me believe that under them innocent hazel eyes, was a bad bitch. Her ex-boyfriend was found dead in his home and I knew that her baby daddy had died I knew this bitch had something to do with it. I could smell a killer from a mile away and this bitch reeked death. When Mya told me, she killed that hoe ass nigga Rashad I wasn't surprised. "What up miss lady long time no see." "Hey Tre thanks for helping take care of my kids." She said. "I need to talk to you about something." Mya spoke up and she sounded scared. Mya my wife was beautiful and innocent. I loved that about her. "Okay bae." She stood up and we walked to the steps going upstairs. I heard some sounds coming from Maurice's room and I assumed he had a friend over. When I went past his room, I had to back track. "Nigga!" I said to him. He looked up and sure as shit it was him The Grim Reaper.

Chapter Two

CRENSHAW

When I saw that nigga Montre I stood up and gave him a handshake. "Thanks for keeping her safe," Tre said to me. I looked at him and nodded. Shit little did he know Aniya had kept me safe. The bitch was a killer and didn't even need me. "No problem." I told him. "I haven't seen or heard anything about you in a while." Tre looked into my eyes. "I had to get out of that lifestyle." I looked him in his eyes trying to read him, but he was cold. "Okay my nigga glad Niya fucking with a real man. I'm gone holla at you I gotta speak with my wife." He said and left with Mya. I breathed deeply once Tre exited the room. The entire time I didn't know what to think. I knew I was going to have to meet up with him. I didn't know if me saving Aniya was going to be a good or bad thing. I didn't owe Tre anything, but with the lifestyle we lived I didn't know if he wanted to kill me. Time would tell, but I wasn't leaving Aniya's side. I sat down on the bed and Mya came back in the room. "Do you need anything to drink?" She asked. I shook my head no. She was a beautiful woman. I wonder did that innocent fresh face of a woman know that she laid next to a killer at night? I wonder did she know that when he said he had to go to work, that nigga was riding through the city reeking-havoc on the entire city? He was a muthafucking maniac in them streets and he used to be my boss. I bet she didn't know and if Montre tried to come at me about anything I was going to make sure his secret was my insurance.

Tre

"What up baby what you want to talk about?" I asked as I closed the door to our bedroom. Mya was beautiful even with her hair in disarray. She looked at me with tears in her eyes. Damn she was always crying. She was so soft but that is what I loved about her. "Baby I am so happy that my best friend is back. She said that we going to have to move. She is going to take the kids, but she asked me to go with her." I let out a sigh of relief damn this was perfect. I needed to move anyway. I did not know that type of lie I was going to tell Mya but shit now

I had the perfect reason. I wrapped my arms around her and held her. As I inhaled her scent I wondered if I would ever be able to be honest with her. I always wondered if she knew who I was would she still love me. "It's okay baby I think this is a great idea." "Really?" She questioned. "Yeah shit you love Niya. It is time for you to bond again with her. I know you missed her, and you would not know what to do without them kids. I know the perfect spot too." I said and she smiled.

Amber

I had to go meet up with Susan. I missed her so much. I hadn't heard from her in a long time. I walked into her office ready to get all my finances and shit together. I knew that no one was out to get me anymore, but I still checked my surroundings. When Susan found out that I was in the office she ended her meeting early. When she saw me, you could see the relief on her face. She gave me a hug. "I am so happy to see you." We embraced for a minute and I held in her scent. We walked into her office and she closed the door. "You look amazing as usual where have you been?" "Living" was all that I said. I didn't know how to tell her all that I had been through. Plus, it wasn't her business. She made that oh really bitch face, but she didn't say anything back to me. "I came to let you know that I will be selling my companies. I have a few buyers so I would need you to draw me up some papers." "Fine" she said without another word. I knew she was pissed. I felt like so what those were Hakeem's companies and I was going to finally get rid of them. Just like I had gotten rid of him. It was time to move on. I still had a lot of shit going on and I knew in any moment the FEDS would be coming to pick me up now that I was out of hiding. I had no problem going to them and telling them that Mr. Richards had killed Dale. I was not about to be in any more bullshit. I had a plan and I was not going to chicken out this time. My kids were most important to me. After selling these companies and talking to the FEDS I was getting the fuck on. Mya and Tre said that they were coming with us when we moved. Tre said that he had the perfect place go. He wanted to go to Victorville, California. I had never been to California, so I was stoked about it. I had sold my companies by the end of the week and my bank account was looking pretty good. Damn I thought to myself I had really done it. I had so much money in the bank that I didn't know what to do with it. I know one thing my kids would never have to worry about anything ever again. I was now a millionaire and not only that, but we were off the hook. Mr. Richards was sentenced to sixty-five years in prison. It was time to move on with my life and do what I was supposed to be doing, being a mother. I loved Crenshaw but this time I was not going to put my all into this relationship. He was a special guy, but years of bullshit I had really shut my heart down. No, I wouldn't leave him, or cheat, or disrespect him but I would never trust him. I would not get my hopes up again like I had done so many times. Lucinda was his sister and she had two boys Luis and Roderick. Her little girl name was Sophia and they were coming with us. I appreciated Lucinda for what she had done for my kids, so I wasn't tripping. Her son Luis was Malcolm's age and Roderick was a year younger than them. Sophia was only six. She was a doll too. I had a family now and she was like a sister to me, her and Mya. It was time to leave all my worries in the past and start over. I needed to stop worrying about what had happened and really enjoy my life. Plus, I was a rich bitch, with a young ass man, two beautiful kids what more could I ask for?

Mya

When we pulled up at the house that Tre said was his property, I was speechless. How in the fuck did he get this property? He was not rich or maybe he was. It was a four-bedroom house with a two car garage in an upscale neighborhood. I loved it from the moment we walked in. I didn't know why he felt that we needed all that space. Tre and I occupied the biggest room. Crenshaw and Amber which is Aniya's name they occupied the other room. Maurice, Luis, and Roderick slept in the same room, and Lucinda got in the room with the girls. It was fun to have so many people in the house because I knew not to long from now, I would be alone. I didn't know what I was going to do with myself since I wasn't going to be working any more. Tre said that I didn't have to work and that he would take care of me. On his salary who was he kidding but I would give it a try. Plus, his salary couldn't be too bad he had this secret house, I pondered about what else he had kept a secret about? 8 years later....

Chapter Three

MAURICE

Cruising through the city a nigga felt like the man. Shit things was going so good for me I didn't know what to do. I made a left at the stop sign and crept through my hood. I never lived in the hood, but this was my hood. After moving to California, we stayed in the same neighborhood as Uncle Tre and Auntie Mya. We moved across the street in a six-bedroom house. Mama loved big ass houses and shit. I loved them too and had grown accustomed to living in big ass houses and nice neighborhoods. To be honest that was all I knew. I never lived in the hood or the ghetto, but when I got introduced to it I instantly fell in love. I was sixteen and my right-hand man Dee had been fucking with me all day talking about how I was a square. Dee lived in the hood so that was all he talked about. Me I had never experienced the shit. I was sixteen driving a fucking old school Chevy with 24s, and a sound system that would shatter a person's windows when I turned it up loud enough. My paint was dripping and shined all year long. I was fine too. I looked just like my father. I had his hazel eyes and I had my hair low cut and it was tapered off on the side. I was 5' 10 light skinned as hell and I had my two fang teeth dipped in gold. I was the man at school and niggas always tried me. Although I didn't live in the hood, I still had those hands. My stepdaddy Crenshaw would take me boxing all the time and I could whoop some ass so wasn't no hoe in me. Niggas they see a pretty boy iced out and the bitches stayed on a nigga and they wanted to try me. After I broke the nigga Rico's nose, they backed the fuck up off me. Rico thought he was so tough hollering that Blood shit. I had to let him know hoe ass nigga I don't give a fuck what hood you from I holds it down. So, when I knocked the nigga out the nigga Dee comes up to me on some fuck boy shit that day. "So, I heard you knocking niggas out Reese?" "Hell, yeah ain't no hoe in me lil nigga" I told him. Dee is a little short nigga, about 5' 4 dark skinned, he had braids. Skinny ass nigga but he would fuck somebody up too, but he wasn't fucking with me. "Alright so you ready to take a trip to the hood?" He joked. This nigga was always trying to get me to ride through the hood with him. I felt like the shit was a setup. I mean at the time Dee and I was not that cool but that day I said fuck it. I told the lil nigga to hop in the ride with me and we headed to his hood. Man, when we got there it was plenty muthafuckas outside. In my neighborhood the only time people be outside is to have barbeques not to just be out here. There were bitches half naked smoking cigarettes. Kids running around outside with no shoes on. It was a crazy sight, yet I loved it. I parked my car and all types of muthafuckas came to my ride I was pissed. They were nosey as hell. I had my pistol with me though. That was one thing my Mama instilled in me. Niggas are grimy. She told me always carry your piece because I don't won't you to get caught slipping. Mama knows best. She was telling the truth. She spoiled me and my sister, gave us whatever we wanted, and I could see the jealous looks in niggas eyes. That day I fell in love with the hood. I mean niggas were cool as fuck and hoes were throwing pussy at me left and right especially when they found out that was my ride. I would fuck all them bitches, but there was one girl that caught my eye. She was a baddie, brown skinned, dreadhead, thick she reminded me of Dutchess off Black Ink Crew she was fine as hell. She didn't even play hard to get neither. Hoes was throwing they ass at me that day. When she came through the spot it was like no one was there except me and her. She was so fucking fine. I tapped Dee on the shoulder. "Who the fuck is that?" I pointed her out. I know that shit was rude, but I didn't give a fuck. I wanted her to know I wanted her. He sucked his teeth "man that's my damn sister Chastity oh hoe ass. You don't want none of that." He made an ugly face. "Man, yes I do." I said. Chastity was older she was nineteen at the time. Her pussy had power and I haven't been right ever since I hit. That is who I was on my way to see now Chastity ole hoe ass. We had been fucking ever since that night and now at the age of twenty I couldn't leave her ass alone no matter what she did. I didn't even bother calling her ass I was just going to pop up at the house fuck it. Chastity thought just because I had dough that I was going to take care of her. I mean I loved that bitch and didn't want to give her up, but man fuck that she was not wifey material. Day after day she proved that she wasn't. I didn't even bother knocking on her best friend Leann door I just walked right in. "Damn nigga you can't knock?" She asked. Leann was a big fine ass bitch too. Light skinned with some deep dimples. She had a fat ass everybody said the bitch looked like Black Chyna I could see it. "Hell, nah where the fuck Chastity at?" I questioned. "In the back sleep" she said. She was braiding some girl hair. I walked past and slapped her ass. I had hit that too. I went to the back and there was Chastity's fine ass laying in Leann's bed naked. I had calmed down a bit. When I thought about how much pain I had been I kicked her ass in her stomach. "AHHHHHH! What the fuck!" She yelled and jumped up. She saw it was me. "Reese what the fuck is wrong with you, nigga?" A naked Chastity asked. "Nah, what the fuck is not right bitch. Your shit hurt don't it? That is how I felt when I pissed bitch your nasty ass done burnt me." She had a stupid look on her face. The other day I went to piss, and my shit burned so bad man I didn't know what to do. Went to the doctor and they told me I had fucking Chlamydia ain't no telling how long I done had that shit fucking around with this hoe. "Nigga that ain't got shit to do with me hell you better talk to one of your other hoes!" She rolled her neck. "My other hoes bitch you the only one I done fucked without a rubber stop playing with me hoe" I was ready to slap her. "Look I am sorry baby I didn't know." She looked sad. "You didn't know! Bitch you out here fucking these niggas raw and then coming to fuck me! That's some nasty ass shit!" I told her. She looked ashamed and she should be. I threw the prescription at her. "Get your pussy right bitch!" I said and headed out the door I had moves to make fuck her nasty pussy ass. She had better been; happy that she was a woman because I really wanted to beat her ass. I should have known she was a nasty bitch. Every nigga with money had practically fucked.

Chapter Four

DANITY

My big brother had me rolling sitting here telling me how he had kicked Chastity today. That was his fault fucking that nasty girl without a rubber, what the fuck did he think. Damn he was going to make me piss on myself. He was looking at me all mad I didn't give a fuck though. I hated staring in his eyes because we had the same hazel eyes. I had long curly hair that went to my ass and my hair was sandy brown. I stood 5'5 and was slender. I had a bit of a butt but these B cup titties were little but that was okay niggas still loved me. I loved being with my brother, but this was not one of those special occasions. "So, what do I owe the pleasure?" I asked. I know he didn't come to tell me about the nasty bitch Chastity. "I got a job for you." "Bet how much?" I jumped at the job. "Damn you gone charge your brother?"

"Hell, yeah nigga shit ain't free." What he thought this was family free day he better take, his ass up the street with that. "Damn Danity okay how about 5 stacks?" "Nope 7"I shook my head. "Damn okay." "What you mean damn okay? Nigga I get paid more than that! Way more than that! So you better be happy you my brother. So, who fucking with my big brother?" "This nigga Pee Wee, this nigga been going around robbing my little niggas thinking it's sweet. Nobody can't get near him man you think you can?" "Don't ever question me nigga I got this shit. I will have it done in a couple hours have my money ready too." I hopped out my brother's Mercedes Benz and went into my Loft. It was beautiful I loved how one of my bedrooms looked over the living room area. I had marble countertops, high ceilings and three bedrooms. It was only me I was a princess, and this was my palace. I went into my dressing room. That is what I called the extra room where I had all my clothes, wigs, jewelry, and shoes. I had a full-length mirror and a vanity. I loved this room this was where I could be whoever I wanted to be and tonight I was going to be Cherry. I put on my short red hair wig. It was cute and simple styled into a bob. I knew exactly where to find Pee Wee. I knew where to find any nigga that was fucking with my brother, I made it my business to keep tabs on these hoe ass niggas. My brother didn't know it, but I had his back before he even asked. I had set some shit up with Pee Wee earlier that day. He was stupid as fuck. I called his phone and pretended I was looking for someone else and his thirsty ass took the bait. I sent him some fake ass pictures of some broad that I Google with her face down and ass up and he was a go. I had called him from a burn out phone so I wouldn't be traced. He had given me the address to his location an hour ago and I told him I would be there at nine. Nah nigga I would be there early. Once I put on my all black outfit with my red wig, I was ready to go. I went two blocks up and three blocks down parked my car in this bar's parking lot and stole a car out the lot. They wouldn't miss it. I drove to the destination got out the car and walked to the door. I knocked on the door and he asked who is it? I didn't give a name I was not about to play no games with Pee Wee. His stupid ass opened the door and I gave him two shots to the head. As quickly as I came, I left. I parked the car back where it was with its newly broken out window and fucked up steering collar. I left a stack of money on the seat and got back in my ride. I was a ghost in the night. Once I got home, I texted Reese that I needed my money and laid in my bed. Killing always drained me even if I didn't do any physical work it drained my mind. Without being able to kill I would go crazy. How did I become this cold stone killer? Good question. I was about fourteen at the time and I was riding with Uncle Tre. Mama had come back for us and we were living with her, but we still had our quality time with Uncle Tre and Auntie Mya. Uncle Tre was taking me to get some candy. I was fourteen but he still treated me like I was a little kid all of them did. Mama stayed in my face, her new boyfriend Crenshaw stayed in my face, Crenshaw's sister Lucinda stayed in my face, Maurice stayed in my face, and definitely Auntie and Uncle stayed in my damn face. We were at a stop light when a black van pulled up on the side of us. I automatically got scared. I got that way ever since that cop had got killed when we were in witness protection. All of a sudden, the doors on the van flew open and before Uncle Tre could react the man was at the driver side window. I know Uncle Tre kept a gun on the side of the passenger side door. I saw the man pull a gun out and before I knew it, I had pulled the gun from the door, and started shooting. My aim was perfect and after I emptied all the rounds from the pistol, I was relieved. I didn't feel sad I felt excited. Uncle Tre made a couple of calls and at first, I thought the police were coming to arrest me, but they came and got the body. After they left, we got back in the car and Uncle Tre turned to me. "How do you feel Danity?" He asked me. He gave me this cold look that I had never seen before. "Okay am I going to jail?" I asked that is what I was worried about. "You don't feel sad?" He probed. I thought about it for a minute. "No, he was going to kill you." I said and Uncle Tre nodded his head and drove to the store. That day opened up everything for me. I learned that Uncle Tre was not a private investigator, but he was a hired killer. He taught me everything I knew. I didn't officially start killing until I turned sixteen. Once I started, I didn't want to stop. I was the clean-up woman.

Chapter Five

MAURICE

"Throw that ass back girl," I said to Chastity as I hit that pussy from the back. It felt like my knees was going to buckle. The shit was feeling too good and on top of that she was throwing that ass back and it was shaking. I grabbed a fist full of her dreads and rammed harder. "Yeaaahhh Daddddy right there please fuck me harder!" She liked when a nigga fucked the shit out of her. I felt myself about to cum, so I pulled out. "What the fuck Rees what you doing?" She asked. "Come suck this dick" she did as she was told and crawled over to me. She swallowed my dick whole and licked the tip. I was ready to explode so I pushed her head back and bust all over her face. She liked that type of shit. Nasty bitch she had a smile on her face. I went to the bathroom and jumped in the shower. It was something about Chastity that made me keep coming back to her ass this was the third time the bitch had burnt me, but I kept coming back. When I got out the shower Chastity was laying in my bed sleep. Nope she had to go. "Chastity!" I yelled waking her up as I walked over to put on my watch. "What baby?" She sounded tired. "It's time for me to drop you off where you going?" "What I thought you was spending the whole day with me?" I turned around and looked at her "why the fuck did you think that?" She rolled her eyes and smacked her lips. "So, we on that now?" She was so fine, but the bitch had to go. I walked over to the bed "hell yeah get your shit on let's go." I could tell she was mad but fuck her. I dropped her ass off and went to my Mom's house to kick it with my stepdad Crenshaw. He was a cool nigga and I loved everything about him. When Moms came back to us, I was happy to see her, but I was happy to see him too. He was the one who saved us. I was only twelve I couldn't do shit, so I was happy that he was man enough to have a heart. Not only was Crenshaw the reason for me being alive but he was the reason that I was the man. When I was sixteen, I called myself trying to smoke weed. Everybody was skipping school so the meet up spot was the park when it was hot enough outside. I call myself smoking weed with my buddies. Crenshaw came smashing down the street. We were all looking like who the fuck is this nigga and what he on. Crenshaw get out of the car "Maurice!" he yelled. I walk over to him. Now I wasn't tripping about him finding out I was skipping school or smoking weed. I wasn't afraid of him. "Get your ass in the car" he said and hopped back in the car. I got in and put on my seatbelt. "So, you think it's okay to be out here smoking weed?" "Yeah" I said, "you do it." I was getting smart and he looked at me like he wanted to punch me in my Adam's apple. "Oh, so your little ass wanna get smart. Since your ass so smart how about being better than me." I didn't have a comeback for what he said so I just shut up. The next day I didn't go to school Crenshaw had booked us a flight. I didn't know where we were going until we got to the airport. He wouldn't tell me nothing as we hopped on the flight to Los Angeles. Crenshaw went to rent a car. We drove through the city and I have to tell you Los Angeles was beautiful definitely something different. We pulled up at this house and there were about five guys hanging on the porch. They were smoking on a blunt. We got out and I was scared for my life. Some guy with tear drops on his face stood up. Crenshaw got out. "What up blood" Crenshaw said. The guy looked at him and smiled "big homie what up?" Crenshaw went in the house and everyone was happy to see him. They all wore red and when they saw that I had on red they were proud. Crenshaw grew up in a foster home and there he got into the street life. Living in Los Angeles, California he had to have protection. Budha that was the only guy name I remember. Budha was the one who had took Crenshaw in and helped him. He taught him everything. He taught him how to shoot his guns and read. He taught him how to roll blunts and play basketball. He taught him how to rob and steal and turned around and told him how to be polite and have manners. Crenshaw had me rolling on the floor laughing when he was telling me this. "Man, Budha would have my ass doing a drive-by and then he would be like 'Shaw blood you don't see that stop sign S.T.O.P. nigga.' Then he would have me rolling a blunt and smoking weed but then we had to go play basketball. That shit did not mix I was out there on the courts tired as a muthafucka. We would be robbing people and he would be like 'ma'am can I please have your purse'?" Crenshaw was funny and I enjoyed myself with his gang that trip taught me just what I needed to know. Stay in school don't be a follower and to do my own thang. Crenshaw was telling me about Budha because he was a leader. Budha taught him how to survive and he was three years younger than Crenshaw. "No matter who you run with, how much clout they got out here on these streets you make sure you are at the top. You want to be a hustler, a street nigga or a fucking send off? I want you to be a hustler all that other shit don't even matter. Being a street nigga don't get you nothing but killed. What I want you to do is make that money and get legit with it. That's one thing your Mama has helped me do become a working man, a businessman. " I knocked on the door and waited for them to open the door. They had a two-bedroom condo. My Mom came to open the door and blessed me with her beauty. Her brown hazel eyes were still beautiful, and she still had her youth. At the age of 44 she still looked good. She grabbed me and hugged me. "My son how are you?" she asked. I kissed her on the cheek and walked past her. It smelled good. "What up Moms I missed you. What you cooking?" I said walking straight to the kitchen. "Some turkey and gravy, dressing, greens, yams, and potato salad." "Dang ma you hungry?" I asked and she started laughing. She was beautiful that smile could light up a room. "Boy Mya, Tre, Lucinda and her kids are coming over." Just then the doorbell rang. I headed to the back. Crenshaw was in the back playing the game, so I joined him. I was a bit mad that Moms had invited Luis over but what could I do this was her house. Luis was Lucinda's son we were the same age and technically cousins. I did not like that nigga though. He was black and Mexican, but he looked more Mexican. He was fat and round with a nasty ass attitude like I was supposed to kiss his ass. The nigga didn't like me because Crenshaw who is his uncle taught me everything I know and not him. The one time when we called ourselves putting the nigga up on some game he fucked around and got caught slanging. We ain't fucked with him since and that was four years ago when I had just got started. He had been working at a cleaning company that my Mom had helped him get. He hated it but his ass wasn't built for the streets. Roderick his brother was a complete nerd who was obsessed with my damn sister. I had to knock his ass out a couple of times I know he be stalking her. Roderick was a pure Mexican he was tall, dark, and had smooth hair. He looked better than his brother, but he had no game. He worked at Game Stop and went to college. He had since got him a girlfriend since I knocked his ass out for looking at my sister too long. Sophia on the other hand was a spoiled brat. She was only fourteen and since my Mother had helped their mother Lucinda start a catering business, she gave Sophia whatever she wanted. I didn't like the little girl she was too damn spoiled. I wanted to beat her ass and make her understand that she wasn't shit just like her damn siblings. Little tramp come to me one day saying some dumb shit. "Maurice, I seen you looking at my ass and the way I am filling out in these jeans." She said. I smacked the shit out of her and dared her to say anything to her brothers because I would have fucked, they ass up too. Shit young ass girl thinking I'm looking at her shit she had better get her mind right had to smack some damn sense in her ass. We were all seated when Uncle Tre and Auntie Mya came in late. This nigga here I thought to myself. Uncle Tre and I had a lo ve/hate relationship I loved him, because he was the man that took care of me when my Mother was gone. He always trea ted me like a son. Shit if I had any problems with the police, I could go to him he would handle it since he a "private inve stigator" please that ol bullshit. Everybody knew the nigga was a killer except Auntie Mya. Mama said that it was be st that we just kept that secret to ourselves it was up to h er to find out. Shit I didn't have a problem with his hidden life shit I could care less. What I did have a problem with was him fucking my little sister. Yes, Danity is 18 now but that don't mean shit! He supposed to look at her like a daugh ter and his filthy ass and banging her back out. Ugh damn I almost vomited from the thought of it. Soon as they walk in the kitchen, he smiles at me. I mug his ass fuck you, nigga. The rest of the dinner was okay fake ass laughs, fake ass stories, and fake ass people. I only came to kick it with my Pops. I wanted to see my Moms I stayed because I needed a home cooked meal. I gave my Mother a kiss good-bye and she walked me to the door. "Love ya son and tell your sister to come by and see me." I shook my head and headed out.

Chapter Six

DANITY

"Damn you still avoiding Mama?" Maurice asked into the phone. I rolled my eyes like he could see me. "Nah Reese I am just falling back a bit. You know get my mind right." "Man whatever" he said and hung up. I looked at my Iphone and started laughing my big brother was crazy. I was naked with just my black bra set on. I was trying to find something to put on so that I could be looking good when my date arrived. I decided on this red dress that fell just above my knees. The split was to die for. I pulled my curly hair into a ponytail and sprayed it with some water. I walked around to let my hair air dry. I decided to paint my toes red since I had time to spare. I hated going on dates, but Julian kept insisting it. He was so annoying, but I loved his little fine ass. Julian was sexy 6'2, built, dark skinned with a chip tooth yes he was fine. I love the way his baritone voice would call my name. I think out of all the guys I was screwing Julian was the one I loved the most. Don't trip Uncle Tre was a good lay but I wasn't in love with him. Hell, I was trying to get rid of his ass. It was a mistake that I have regretted since day one. It was after my 18th birthday. I had done a job on these twin girls that were going to snitch on some drug lord out. I had just got home, and Uncle Tre was sitting in front of my apartment building. "Hey Unc what you doing here so late?" I asked. He had that glossy look like he was about to cry oh fuck I hated to see people cry. I had stopped crying a long time ago, so it felt awkward to watch a person cry. I didn't know what to do. "Mya, she trying to leave me." He said as he followed me into my house. "She said that I am staying out too late and she is tired of it. She thinks I am cheating." "Well, are you?" I asked as I screamed from my bedroom. "No!" He yelled back. I came back in the living ro om with my white robe o n. I loved everything to be in white. My entire house was white. White Ashley furniture set, white kitchen table, white bedroom set, white bathroom set, white everywhere I liked to feel pure. I sat next to Uncle Tre. "Well Unc all I can say is she tripping. Just tell her what you do she can't get mad about it." He laughed "easy for you since you are my worker. Mya can't know that I am out there hunting people down killing them. She cannot know that I am the most highly paid assassin in the world. Hell, I have millions in the bank. I don't even know where it is going to go because I don't want to over-spend, scared Mya will find out." "Well you know you can give me some of that cash a sistah can never have enough money." I said and we laughed. "Dan, how does it feel to be a grown woman?" He questioned. "It feels great." I told him even though I felt no different. The mood had changed I could tell he was absorbing my smell. I loved the way I smelled like vanilla. Wasn't nothing like taking milk baths in the daytime. I loved to take milk baths and put a little honey in my milk. Water just was not enough to wash away my sins. "Have you been fucked by a grown man yet?" Uncle Tre was straight forward but I liked that about him. I was straight forward too. At that moment I forgot that he was married to my Mama's best friend. I forgot that he was like a father figure. I stood up and opened my robe. My pierced titties set up perky and alert and my shaven pussy was I am sure a sight. "Nah why you trying to show me?" That night Uncle Tre fucked me in all types of positions. I rode that dick from the back. He licked the crack of my ass to the front of my pussy. He sucked my toes and licked my nipples. Oooh how I begged for more. I straddled him and rode him like a horse I bounced up and down on that dick. It was good I squirted, I came, I shook, and had multiple orgasms. That was the last time we had sex that was over a month ago. I had not had sex with him anymore, but those images still play in my head. Uncle Tre fucked the shit out of me. I really wanted more, I wanted him to divorce Auntie Mya and run away with me. For days after I was going crazy, I didn't know what to do. I called my big brother and told him to come over. When I told Reese about what I had done he smacked the shit out of me. I would have killed his ass let it had been someone else. "Danity you stupid as hell I know you know better. I hate that this shit is going on. Tre ass don't love you he came over here crying to you about his wife who he loves. You was just a quick lay and you over here talking about you think you in love sit your dumb ass down girl." Maurice was right and after that I went ahead and never mentioned the sex neither of us did. We always met in public places so that it could not happen again but on my lonely nights I think about those earth shattering orgasms. I was set as I put my curly hair down around my face. Julian wanted to meet at the Cheesecake Factory. Hell, whatever I did not care I was hungry and wanted to eat. I should have gone to my Mom's house, but I was scared that she might see the guilt in my eyes. When I pulled my white on white Cadillac up in the parking lot, I was mad as hell that there was not a parking spot close to the door. I had on these six-inch stilettos. I loved wearing heels made my 5' frame seem taller. I finally made it inside and told the host I was with Murphy. She pulled me to the back as the others who were waiting stared and looked pissed. There he was in a back booth looking sexy as ever. Julian was so sexy to me. He was about 23 and he was a trained shooter. He killed for a living too. He smiled and got up and let me in. Damn what a gentlemen. I had met Julian at a conference while I was trying to get this target. She was a white schoolteacher by day and a damn pedophile by night. I guess that they had hired on Julian and I just in case one of us missed the target. I had noticed him stalking the woman and I was getting angry. I know he noticed me so when I gave him that look, I knew what was up. They had wanted to take one of us out who I don't know. When they hire two assassins to do a job then one of your times are up. I had only been in the game for about two years, so I knew at the time that it wasn't me or was it? To this day I still don't know who is supposed to be killed but we watch our backs very closely. I have asked Uncle Tre does he know anything about what is going on but he plays stupid. Our dinner was good with light conversation and flirting. Afterwards I followed Julian to his house. As soon as we got to the door, I was on him. He had a contract out in Paris for the last three months. This was our first time seeing each other since then, and I wanted him so badly that I could barely speak. I had enough energy to tell him "fuck me" and that is what he did for three hours. Damn he was like the energizer bunny he just kept going.

Chapter Seven

MAURICE

W hy do people have to be so fucking stupid? My big brother Junior was a pure fuck up and he was getting on my nerves. The nigga was damn near ten years older than me and was acting like a young nigga. Now my other two brothers Chris and Jon-Jon I never had no problems with them but Junior he was testing me. "Junior this ain't all the money. How the fuck you want to re-up but you short? My connect is not gone take this. I tell you that shit every time." I said as I kept recounting his money. "Man tell your, connect that I don't give a fuck. That wasn't no gas that shit was some fucking huff tell that fuck boy that." I didn't even say shit I threw the money on the table and exited the house. I looked just like my brother Junior. Same eyes and everything he was just a bit taller than me. He was my identical twin damn near, but we were total opposites. They had moved out to California where we were once they got grown. They Grandmother had died, and we were the only family they knew. I know the nigga didn't like me. We were brothers that was the only reason I was allowing his bitch ass to talk to me like that. I met up with Dee to talk business. We were meeting at Wendy's parking and of course the dirty ass nigga was late. I felt like the nigga was feeling some type of way about me. I know I was fucking his sister but so what. I think that he was salty at me because at Danity's 18th All White Affair birthday party I saw him eyeing my little sister. I knew Danity had sex, but she wasn't about to be fucking him. Plus, Danity had more dough than me shit so Dee was not on her level. This rat face ass nigga grabbed her hand and I told his ass like nigga you got the wrong idea about my sister. Hoe ass nigga talking about man you fucking my sister. His damn sister a known hoe shit. So, I know that he kind of salty because the nigga had been acting shady lately. "What up nigga" I jumped into Dee's 2014 Dodge Challenger. "Shit nigga muthafuckas want to know what is going on with your, connect?" "What you mean?" I questioned. "Niggas basically want to know who your connect is?" He explained blowing his stanking ass cigarette in my face. I took offense to that shit and wanted to beat his ass, but I kept a cool head. "Why the fuck they worried about that shit muthafuckas need to make this money!" I yelled. "Alright I was just saying niggas being nosey." He said. The look on his face was simple no emotion I couldn't read the nigga. What the fuck was he on? I jumped out of the car hurriedly got in my ride. I had kept my car on and pulled off. I didn't know what the fuck was going on but for some reason I didn't trust Dee. Why the fuck was niggas worried about my connect? The only reason they would want to know who the fuck my connect was is if they wanted to knock the middleman, out of the way. From what I knew and what they knew I was the middleman. Yeah, I knew what it was. I was driving and thinking so much that I didn't even notice the light had changed to a red light and I rammed into a purple minivan. Damn! I jumped out of the car. Good thing I always kept my seat belt on. I didn't hit the van hard, but my right head light was damaged. The minivan wasn't really damaged but I wanted to make sure the person in the car was alright. As soon as I was about to walk to the driver side this light skinned beauty got out of the car. She was 5'2, light skinned, with gold dreads. She had a little piercing in her left nostril she was fine, and I forgot I had hit her. "Damn nigga you gone have to pay for this shit." She yelled at me. I smiled she was fine, and I loved a bitch with dreads for some reason "shit I can do you one better how about I just buy you a new car." I said She looked at me like I was full of shit and rolled her eyes "what is your insurance information?" "Oh you think a nigga playing?" I pulled out my phone and dialed my homie up real, quick. I was looking at her and she was still looking mad and she looked a bit cold. As the phone was ringing, I whispered to her "go get in my ride baby girl get out the heat." She was looking at me like I was crazy, but she did as she was told. "Aye nigga come get this car for me I just got in an accident." The caller said a simple okay. I ran over to my car and got in. As soon as I stepped in the car her fragrance hit me. "Damn ma what you got on?" I asked. "Minajesty so umm can I get your car insurance information?" She asked again and pulled out her phone. I looked her up and down. She was a petite little thing but when she walked past to get in the car, I saw that she had a fat ass. She had a little gap in between her teeth she was sexy as hell. "Didn't I just tell your ass we about to go get you a car?" I asked. I had to get a bit aggressive with her because she was taking me as a joke. "Who the fuck you talking too?" She snapped. I had to laugh. Good thing my Pops was pulling up with his tow truck. Shit Moms and Pops owned damn near everything in this damn city and if they didn't have any parts, they knew the owner. He knocked on my window. I got out of the car. "What up Pops I ran into the nice lady car" I pointed at the dreadhead beauty as she sat in the car. Pops just shook his head and went to her window. She opened her door. "Sorry about his fuck up sweetie. I am his Daddy and he gone go get you another car. Get any ride at the lot." "Oh no sir it is fine it is just a little bump. I will be okay I will just call my insurance company." I walked over to the side of the car where they were talking "you see Pops she a difficult one." "Babygirl you are about to get a brand-new car fuck an insurance policy. That way your premium won't go up and my son won't go up. What your name sweetheart?" "Imani Dillard" "Okay Imani my son about to take you to get a new car." She didn't say anything I see she had calmed down on the insurance shit. It was my pleasure to buy her a car. I didn't know her like that, but I wanted too. "You alright Ms. Imani?" I asked as I hopped back in the driver's side. My dad was putting her van on the tow truck. "Yes, I am good" she said. My dad came over back to the car. "What's your address sweetie?" She told him the address and he wrote it down. "Okay have fun car shopping."

Chapter Eight
IMANI

This nigga was so fucking fine and he knew it. I didn't even like men but this fine ass nigga next to me could get it. Damn, I wanted to run my hands through his head. I had been a lesbian since I was fourteen and I had never been with a man. As of right now I was single because I couldn't even find the right woman. I looked over at the man and I had to ask his name. "So you got a name?" "Oh yeah Maurice sweetie" he said back to me. I settled in my seat. I had been on my way home after dropping off my daycare children. I was just starting out and I was pissed that he had hit me, but I was grateful that none of my kids were with me. As we pulled into the car lot, I was surprised it was all new cars in the lot. I didn't really think he was going to buy me a new car but hell I was going because they insisted. We got out the car and I allowed the California sun to beat down on me. I had my dreads in a bun and I knew I looked good. Men had always hit on me because I was a fem and they thought that I wanted them, but I didn't. As we made our way to the entrance of the car lot, it was looking like no one was there it was after hours. To my surprise he opened the office. I wondered did he own this car lot. "I'm gone let you get warm lil mama. So, what kind of car are you looking for anyway?" He asked. We walked into the back office and he turned up the air conditioner. "Well that was my transportation van for my daycare that I just started." I sat down. "Oh, damn I am sorry so we looking for a van huh, Ms. Entrepeneur." My cellphone went off and I looked down and it saw that it was Shanita my ex. I ignored her and sent her ass to voicemail. She was a nasty bitch. "That your man?" he asked. "Nah my ex-girlfriend." I had to let him know that I was not interested in men. The look of shock on his face was evident "girlfriend oh damn that's all I got to compete with yeah you gone be mine." I rolled my eyes "so where the vans? Am I going to have to pay a monthly fee or something?" "Damn girl I told you I am about to buy you a car damn, no car note, no nothing." I just couldn't believe he was going to buy me a car, but I went along with the shit. I picked out a white 2015 Dodge Caravan and I loved it. He did the paperwork for me and gave me some temporary tags. He set me up in my new car. "Okay Ms. Imani you all set okay. I am sorry about that shit." He was sweet and I really appreciated him buying me this ca r. He handed me his card. "If you need me for anything call me especially if you start feeling men make sure your fine ass call, me." I had to laugh he was arrogant, but I liked it. I made it to my house safe and sound. My apartment was empty and quiet. I pulled off my clothes and got in the shower it had been a long day. As the hot shower ran down my body and I listened to Pa ndora I thought about Maurice. Damn I ha d never felt thi s way about a man what was happening to me? I got out the shower and laid across my bed naked. I drifted off to sleep. The next morning my alarm woke me up at 5am I had to get dressed and go get my kids. I got dressed into my blue jeans, and white green shirt. I was about to head out the door when the doorbell rang. I went to the intercom and pushed the button. "Who is it?" I could not think of who could be at my house this early in the morning. "Maurice, I brought you the car seats out of your van and your personal shit" I buzzed him up. I opened the door to my apartment and waited out in the hall. As soon as I saw his sexy ass, I started to get moist. Damn he was so fine he just did something to me. "What up Imani I just wanted to bring yo stuff." I couldn't even say anything he was so damn fine. Just then my house phone buzzed, and I knew it was my best friend Kim'Esha. I didn't even answer him I just went in the house to answer the phone. I needed to take my mind off of how fine he was. "Hello." "Bitch I am waiting" Kim'Esha sounded annoyed in the phone. "I am coming boo" I said and hung up the phone. Maurice had let himself into my apartment. "That was one of your girlfriends?" He sounded jealous "nah my best friend I have to pick up her kids." "Okay I won't hold you up lil mama. I know you say you don't like men, but can you just give me one chance to take you out and show you what you missing?" I looked at him he was fine and to be honest I didn't need a date to know what I was missing. Shit the sight of him was making feel some type of way that I had never felt. "Sure, Maurice just check with me this weekend. We can do something, but I have to go." I looked at him and noticed he didn't have anything in his hand for the first time. "Where the stuff that was in my car?" I locked my house door. "That shit outside I wasn't about to carry that shit upstairs hell I will put it in the car when we get outside." "Right." I responded as we headed out.

Chapter Nine
DANITY

I had to meet with Uncle Tre, and I was not looking forward to the shit. We were meeting at the food court in the mall. I dressed in a long shirt that with some leggings that covered up my body. I didn't want him to look at me. I knew this shit was inevitable, but I wanted to make sure it was all professional. As I made my way to the food court, I saw Uncle Tre. Damn he was fine chocolate as ever. A damn chill went up my spine and my pussy exploded with juices. I had to stop in mid walk to calm myself. My mind kept flashing back to the way he licked my ass that night, damn. I gathered my composure and walked to where he was seated. "What up Dan you been avoiding me?" "Nah I just been busy," he nodded his head. "I got a new assignment for you. It is out of town in Miami. This the information you have five days. Don't miss."

He said as he got up from the table. The nerve of his ass I never missed a damn target. I grabbed the file and made my way back to my car. I got in car and was not surprised that Uncle Tre was sitting in my passenger seat. "What Tre?" I asked. "You don't miss me Danity?" I looked at his face and could not believe he asked me that shit. He was my Uncle well my Mother's best friend husband and I could not do this. "As an Uncle and mentor yes, as a fuck buddy no." I crossed my arms across my chest. "Alright that is fair" he got out of my car. I was not a bad person and I was not about to add being a damn adulterer to my list of sins. I started my car up and I felt my phone ring. That Ciara "I bet" started playing and I knew right away it was Tip. Tip was the finest nigga and my damn weakness. He was dark as midnight and stood at 5'9. Bitches were afraid of him but not me we were a match made in heaven. On the streets they called him Black, his government was Omar Fitzgerald but to me he was Tip. Yup Tip because when the tip of his dick touched the outside of my pussy I exploded. He was my main man and he was Uncle Tre's right-hand man. "Hello" I answered the phone as sexy as possible. "So, what the fuck the nigga Tre talking about?" "He just got a job for me baby" I knew Tre had told him that he was meeting me. The only person who knew about Tip, Julian, and Uncle Tre was my brother Maurice he was everything to me and I told him everything. "Oh, okay baby girl when you leaving?" "Tomorrow morning," I turned my car on and headed to my brother's house. "Oh, okay hit me up when you get back." "Alright big daddy." We disconnected the call. I made it to Maurice's house in no time. I used my key to get in his house. I had made sure to put the file in my bag. I locked the door behind me and went into his office. I made a copy of all the information and set it on his desk. I always left my destination and who I was going to take out with my brother. I trusted him with my life and if anything happened to me, I know he would stop at nothing to get revenge. My mark was an easy target. Hell, I didn't even stay in Miami for five days. I had braided my hair to the back and put on my blonde long lace front. Smiley was his name and he was a drug dealer that did not want to pay his "taxes." The thing about my job was I worked for dirty cops that Uncle Tre knew. They had all types of muthafuckas on the payroll to the point where shit was not traceable, and bodies were not found. I went to the club where he frequented, and it was so easy to catch his eye. He was a big nigga, but he was fine as hell. Light skinned, long ass hair that he had in a ponytail, he was sexy. I had on some little ass shorts that had my ass cheeks hanging out. I made sure to wear white to make me look a bit thicker. I danced and drank my Coca Cola I never drank on a job. I made eye contact with him. I smiled and played with my tongue ring. He smiled and he pushed the thick ass girl off him. She was gorgeous too and I damn near wanted her. I made my way over to him because shit if he pushed her off him then he wanted me. "Come home with me" he whispered in my ear. Ugh his breathe smelled of alcohol. I didn't say anything as I grabbed his fingers and put them in my mouth. I sucked on them one by one. His homeboys looked on in envy, but they just didn't know that they should be grateful that I had not come for them. "Damn lil mama" he got excited. Shit after that he didn't even stay to the end, we headed out to the parking lot. I purposely made sure Charm dropped me off. That was my homegirl and sometimes she went with me. She didn't know what I was doing. I told her I wanted to visit Miami and she could come for free. I told her to drop me off down the street so that she wouldn't know I was going to the club. Shit she was there just to make sure I had a ride. I made sure she was at another club. As we hopped into Smiley's Range Rover, I knew this was going to be easier than I thought. When we got to his house, he was drunk. I sat on his couch and let him talk. He wasn't talking about shit and I was ready to get the shit over with. I didn't even know where I was. I saw that he had placed his keys right on the table. Good shit I needed a ride home. He went to the bathroom to piss. I positioned myself and as soon as he hit the corner of the living room, I let off three shots right to the face. His life was over. I grabbed the keys off the table and was on my way out the door. Just when I was about to walk out the door two of his homeboys were walking in. I let off five more rounds and ended their lives. Damn my heart was racing I was hoping there was no one else coming. I should have at least waited. This nigga thought they were about to party me. I made my way out the door and went to the Range Rover. I started it up and as I sped away, I saw two more cars headed to Smiley's house and I was happy that I had gotten the fuck out of there. That was a close call. When I made it to the hotel Charm was still gone. I texted her and told her I had made it back to the hotel and to enjoy herself. I fell asleep just like I always did after killing the shit exhausted me.

Chapter Ten

TRE

I had to have a meeting with my boss, and I knew that it was serious. I kissed my precious wife before I left her. We had just left the doctor that morning and they had confirmed our worst nightmare, she was dying of cancer. There was nothing we could do about it she was going to die, and no amount of money could buy me out of this fatal illness. I knew it was karma coming for my ass, but I was fucked up about it because it was hurting my Mya. She had been suffering over the years with cancer. It was a year after things had settled down with Aniya. She found a lump in her breast, we did chemo. Everything was fine until a couple of months ago. This time the cancer came back and it had spread tremendously throughout her body. There was nothing the doctor could do. Her fate was sealed. I loved Mya and that is why I lied to her about my dealings with the underworld. Mya was a precious jewel that was not to be corrupted. The tears stung my eyes as I thought about my beautiful wife, but I had to make this meeting. I didn't want to leave her as she walked into the house alone. I was going to be right back and tend to her emotional needs. As I stepped into his office, my face turned into stone. "Look I need to know who the fuck is the plug that is taking over the weed game." My boss got right to business immediately. Weed, marijuana, Mary jane, gas, loud, kush, whatever you wanted to call it was making its way through the city like crack and heroin. Niggas loved to smoke and shit it was absolutely necessary for niggas to get them a blunt. Over the last couple of years weed had been the biggest drug sold and my boss wanted parts of it. He was the top and he never missed an opportunity to get more money. That is what he did he wanted a piece of the pie whether it be legal or illegal. He wanted parts. "I don't even think the nigga is from the city." I was not interested in finding out this information. "I don't give a fuck if he from Chicago or Alaska find out who the fuck he is!" He growled. "Alright damn." I retorted. I left his office and didn't even think about what he had just said. I had other things on my mind like my wife dying. Damn I couldn't handle this and on top of that Danity was avoiding me. I mean if I didn't have

Mya then next in line would be Danity once Mya died, I wanted Danity to settle down with me. I know I shouldn't be thinking about that type of shit but hell I had to think for the future. I had been dealing with death since I was a kid. My mother was a killer she killed my father in cold blood because she found out he was a crackhead. She did not give a fuck and she told the police that she wanted to take him out of his misery. Before that my father was a damn drug lord who flooded the city with the best but somehow his luxury became a necessity. I grew up in foster care my sister and I. Latonya was my older sister and after year of being in foster care she got killed. They say the group home that she was living at caught on fire. I was alone in this world except Mya. I made my way through high school and majored in criminal Justice that is where I met the corrupt officers and judicial officials. Those were some of the most corrupt people in the city and they paid me well to clean the city. Crenshaw I had met him and he wasn't ready to be a killer. I had let him leave without killing him because I knew that he was a real nigga. I never thought I would see him again, but it was nice to see that Aniya had settled down with a nice nigga like him. He was hard but soft hearted. I needed to find out who was running shit in the weed department on the streets. I hadn't even thought about the shit until my boss had brought it up. Shit it was like a piece of money we were missing. I couldn't even understand how we didn't know how we didn't know who the plug was. I made my way back to the house and I as I made my way to our bedroom, I could hear my wife's cries. That shit broke my heart and I wanted to turn around and drown myself in liquor, but my selfish ways were the reason that she was in this predicament. I believed in karma and that is why I never wanted to have children. I didn't want my kids to pay for my sins but now I saw my wife was going to suffer because of me. She had been experiencing excruciating pain in her head. She would wake up crying. We went to the doctor to find out she had brain cancer. That shit was a shock and it hurt my heart. When Mya found out the news, she let out a scream that came from the soul. She was hurt and her life would be soon over, and she didn't understand why. That scream was the most disturbing thing I had ever heard. I had killed kids, old people, families, mothers, fathers, and even a pastor and they all had a different plead in their eyes or a scream that came from their mouth. Nothing I mean nothing could prepare me for the hurt that my wife was going through. When I walked into the room Mya was laying in the bed just crying. I walked over to her and held her. "Baby did you talk to your sister Monica?" "Yessss" she said through her tears. "Oh Lorrrd why?" She cried. I felt so hurt and I just couldn't deal with it. Mya was my everything I just laid there and help her. I inhaled her scent this beautiful woman was going to die, and I couldn't do anything to stop it. For many years I had taken life and I couldn't do anything to stop the inevitable of my wife's death. Oh, how the world works. I was trying to be God, but God was showing me who was really boss. As soon as Mya fell asleep, I got out of the bed. I got in my car and rode the 30 minutes to Amber's house. I didn't know why Aniya, Malcolm, and Deena didn't keep their names when the cops were not looking for her, but that was their decision I guess they wanted a change. As I pulled into the driveway, I saw that it was after midnight. I knew that it was late, but I needed to talk to her. I knocked on the door and waited. It was dark at fuck. I heard his voice and I looked down at my chest there was a red dot. Once a reaper always a reaper, I thought "it's me Crenshaw, Tre." I heard the door opening as he peeped out "why you here so late?" "It's Mya she has brain cancer." I had to let him know I was serious. He had no reason to think that I was coming to kill him. He also knew my job and shit could change in a matter of hours because when your life was marked then it was over. He opened the door and let me in. He walked to the back and I knew that he went to go get his wife. After about ten minutes

Amber appeared just as beautiful as always. Amber had always been beautiful to me, but she wasn't pure like Mya. I know that for a fact it was something in her eyes that led me to believe that she was not to be fucked with.

Chapter Eleven

AMBER

I couldn't believe this muthafucka had the nerve to show up at my house alone. When Crenshaw told me that Mya had brain cancer, I threw on some clothes and hurried down the stairs. I knew about him sleeping with my daughter Danity and to be honest I was hurt like he was my husband. I couldn't understand Danity but she had always been rather distant with me. At the age of 18 she got up and left home. I knew everything that is what they didn't know. I knew Tre was a killer, I knew about Crenshaw's involvement, I knew about Danity working for Tre, I knew about my damn son Maurice too. They thought because I wasn't in the streets that I didn't know shit, but one thing is a mother knows. After all the shit I had been through I had to snoop. Crenshaw had told me a lot about his past and he also told me about my son. Maurice sitting there telling me he was going to school for chemistry damn lie! I knew it was going to be some shit with Tre and Danity because they were too close. When I confronted him, he told me about the hired killings, but I knew it was something more to their relationship. I had wanted to talk to my daughter about it, but her ass had been avoiding me. I didn't want my best friend to be hurt because she had done so much for me and my kids, but my loyalty lied with my children. They weren't the best and Lord knows I was far from the perfect person. I couldn't blame them it was my fault too. I had killed and I had to do what I had to in life. If that is what Danity thought was going to fulfill her life then fine, but I didn't know if Tre had pressured her into it or what. I sat across from Tre and looked into his eyes. He was sad I could tell. "We got the results back and she has brain cancer. There isn't anything we can do but wait for her to be called home" he started crying and his body shook with grief. I was sad to know that my best friend in the whole world was going to die. I had been hit with death so much that I was numb until it actually happened. I felt sympathy for him, so I got up and consoled him. I hugged him and it made me want to cry but I couldn't my heart was too cold. After talking with Tre a little bit more he left and I went upstairs to my husband. I tossed and turned the entire night thinking of my best friend. Damn she was such a good person and after all the dirty shit I had done you would think why things like this hadn't happened to me. I had drifted off to bed and my body woke up at its usual time six am. I dragged myself to the bathroom I felt fucked up like I had been drinking all night. I looked at the mirror and splashed the water across my face. Damn I looked-liked my mother Lisa. The older I got I looked more and more like her. That wasn't a bad thing neither, as I got older, I actually got slimmer. I still kept my hair in a short cut I loved everything about me. I had started dying my hair black because the gray was evident. I wondered where my husband Crenshaw was. I loved me some Crenshaw and after doing shit so wrong with so many men I had finally gotten it right with him. He was my everything and he treated my kids like his own. I loved his relationship with Maurice. I turned the water on extra hot because I needed to drown my sins from my body. I loved the way the water hit my body. I was not about to cry I was going to stay strong. I walked to my bedroom wrapped in my towel and looked in my walk-in closet for something to wear. Over the years I had drowned my wardrobe in black but today I was going to brighten this day up. I found a yellow sweater and some green jeans. I know the shit sound crazy but when you from Wisconsin you can't do shit but rep Green Bay. Plus, that was Mya's favorite team and I know that it would put a smile on her face. I looked good and I applied a little lipstick and lip liner on my eyes and set to get out the door. When I made it, downstairs Crenshaw was at the table counting stacks of money. I didn't even bother and ask him where he got the shit from. I kissed him on the cheek and let him know I was going to check on Mya. The thirty-minute drive was a breath of fresh air. It was still rather cold in Milwaukee, so I had my heat on blast in my new 2015 Chrysler. I was just testing it out to see if I was going to buy it, but I think I wanted the Infinity. I pulled into the driveway and didn't see Tre's truck his ass bet not be with my daughter. I made my way to the house and knocked on the door. I was hoping that Mya would answer and to my surprise she did, and she was alert and happy. Mya's skin was still beautiful. She had a colorful scarf to hide the bald spot that was in the middle of her head. I could see why Tre was so smitten with my daughter because her and Mya did look alike. However, my daughter was an 18-year old teenager as far as I was concerned, and his old ass had no reason to be fucking on her. I hugged my friend and inhaled her scent. "Hey girl" she said. "I am surprised to see you." I walked in and sat on her white couch. "Yes, Tre came by last night and told me the news about you going to the doctor." She sat across from me "well of course and I was so damn sad." I saw the tear slip from her eyes. "Today though is a new day, Niya. I have lived and now I must die." She was the only one who I allowed to call me Niya her and Crenshaw. At times I forgot that life I had once lived as Aniya Turner. I went over to her and brushed that tear away. "I don't know how you feel, and I won't lie to you I would be scared as hell. I am so happy that you are taking it so well. I know you scared Mya, but I am here." She grabbed me and hugged me tight. I knew she was scared and was putting up a front. She grabbed me so tight and cried so hard that her body shook. I know my shirt was soaked with tears and snot but that was okay because I wanted her to know that I was here for her. After about twenty minutes of crying she finally stopped. "I needed to let that out," she laughed. We sat in silence for a minute "you want to go get a massage and go to the spa?" I asked. "Yeah sure that sounds great." She went to get on her clothes as I sat and watched Oprah. I heard the door open and in walked Tre. I really had mixed feelings about him. He was an okay guy but at the same time he had corrupted my little Danity. I know she had a mind of her own, but I really wanted to know if she wanted to be a hired assassin. That shit just didn't sit well with me. Yes, I had killed yes, I had pulled the trigger, but it was necessary, and it was for me. She was killing for money and for other people. "Hey Amber you here to check up on Mya?" "Yea we gone go to the spa and get pampered." I smiled. "Thanks." "No need to thank me she been my friend before you met her." I let him know. Mya came downstairs and we headed out to pamper ourselves. I know she didn't have a long time, but I wanted her to enjoy herself until she was bed ridden. My phone started ringing and I saw that it was Quita my kid's auntie. I rolled my eyes and pressed ignore. Sooner or later I was going to have to kill this bitch because she was getting on my nerves. Ever since she had gotten out of jail some stupid person had given her my number like we were best friends. The fuck it could have been anyone but the day that she called me and answered I let that bitch know that I was not to be fucked with. "Hello," I answered the unknown number. "Hey this Aniya?" She asked. I paused because no one called me Aniya unless they knew me. "Yeah who is this?" "Chiquita" she said, and I damn near lost control of my car. "Who the fuck gave you my number?" I probed as I gained control of myself. She laughed "oh you don't want to talk to me sister in law?" "Bitch please you was planning on killing me what the fuck do you want?" I had pulled my car over by this time. "I want money I am broke and just got out of jail. I did the whole bid with nothing and I need money." "Bitch you got me fucked up I am not about to give you none of my money." "My brother left you all that money and you not gone give me none bitch you got me fucked up!" She yelled into the phone. I wasn't even about to argue with the ignorant bitch. "You know what Chiquita when you ready to die bitch you come see me. Until then choke your fat ass on a chicken bone and die." I hung my damn phone up. She had called me a couple of times after that, but I never had answered. Whenever that bitch found out my address, she would have a damn surprise waiting on her ass. I was going to shoot to kill and believe I never miss my target.

Chapter Twelve

MAURICE

Although Imani had told me that she was into women I didn't give a fuck I was going to still hang out with her. She seemed cool as fuck. I had texted her and asked if she played basketball and she responded duh so I told her we could go to the gym to play a little ball. Chastity had been blowing up my phone and I had been ignoring her ass. I really liked Chastity it was just something about the girl, but she was a hoe and I couldn't do anything with her. The only thing I could do was fuck her I couldn't build with her. I never told anyone my business so that is why muthafuckas really did not know who I was. I am Maurice Moore better known as Reese. To these niggas I was the middleman that's all they knew. After I came back from L.A. with Crenshaw, I had put my plan in motion with him. I had gathered enough information and was about to become the next up and coming kingpin. Crack was out of my lead, Crenshaw showed me how to grow my own weed. I had my very own greenhouse full of different strains that I had grown over the years. Where I kept the weed and because of his idea I was damn near a millionaire. No one knew where I got the weed from all they thought was I had a connect out in Cali. Nah I didn't want anyone to know that I was the connect, I was the plug to that good green. Weed was the new drug and I was the nigga who supplied majority of California streets. I also had expanded to Wisconsin, Michigan, New York, and North Dakota.   Niggas had been trying to see where I had got that fire ass weed from and I would just let them know it was my connect. These stupid ass niggas were paying me double for being the middleman and the connect. I was pocketing all that shit and I worked by myself. Shipments I worked that shit, I had a schedule because I told niggas my connect was an organized muthafucka. I had a warehouse here in the city where I had weed too but I made sure nobody knew where my shit was at that no one knew what I was doing. The only person who knew about this was my Pops Crenshaw and my little sister Danity. They were the only people who I trusted. I mean I trusted my Moms, but I just wasn't ready to tell my Moms about the shit that I did. She thought I was going to school for Chemistry yeah, I was in the lab inventing new weed, stronger loud, and making that gas stanky. How things were going the new laws being passed I was going to eventually be legit, but right now I was waiting for the opportunity. I met Imani at the gym, and she was looking good as hell. I had on some True Religion jeans, but I had my basketball shorts underneath. She had on some little ass black shorts that looked like they were for yoga or some shit. Yeah, she definitely wanted a nigga, but she just wanted to play. I walked up on her and kissed her on her mouth. It was just a little peck, but you could tell that she loved every moment of it. She was anticipating more but I pulled away. "What up sexy you ready for me to whoop that ass?" Her sexy ass smirked "boy bye I am cold at this game." "Yeah we'll see." Man, I tell you I had played with many niggas. I loved the game of basketball, but I had to admit she was cold at the game. She was damn near like Sanaa Lathan in Love and Basketball Imani had game. After she had started embarrassing my ass, I called it quits she was killing me. "I see you couldn't hang." She laughed as I walked her to her car. I was glad she had put on her some sweatpants because I noticed a couple of them niggas looking at her ass. "Nah I was just letting you win." We both started laughing shit we knew that was a lie. She was killing my ass. I had to admit that I liked her even more. She was like a nigga in a woman's body she turned me on. "So, you been enjoying your new van?" She unlocked her doors and got in "hell yeah the kids love it too thanks so much." "Whatever you need baby girl I will give it to you just ask." I said. "Well since you said that can I have five hundred dollars?" She put her hand out. I didn't even hesitate I started going in my pockets to retrieve the money when she stopped me. "Maurice I was just playing" she was laughing, and I couldn't stop looking at those pretty ass teeth. "You are sweet, but I don't need anything you have done enough." I was speechless no one had ever stopped me from giving them money. She saw that I was a bit shocked and she grabbed my shirt and kissed me. That kiss sent fireworks through my body and I knew that she was the one for me. She pulled away first and I was sitting there wanting more. She started laughing "don't think you getting no pussy nigga I just wanted to see how those lips felt." I nodded my head and let her drove off I knew what was up, she wanted a nigga. I turned my phone back on as I walked to my car. I had ten missed messages from Dee. I know that nigga was mad because of the little talk we had the other day in the parking lot, but he was out of pocket. I looked at the text messages and he was acting like a bitch. Dee

'Reese nigga wud up' Dee 'nigga is u gone get my package for me or wat??' I had completely stopped fucking with this nigga, and I had every right too. He was making me wonder and I did not like to wonder. I was glad I stopped fucking with his sister too. Shit to be nice I called that nigga. My car was hooked up to my phone. I dialed his number and the speakers blared I turned the shit down. "Hello" his hoe ass answered quick as hell. "What up nigga?" He sounded desperate. "Shit nigga I been calling you since last week I need to re-up the fuck going on?" "You are acting suspect Dee" I told him. "What the fuck you mean nigga?" He snared. "Meet me around the corner from the Hood." I ended the call. I made sure to text Danity my location I needed her ass on stand-by just in case this nigga was on some fuck shit. I didn't need an entire team my sister was a cold-hearted killer and I loved her to death. She texted me back and said she was already there. How the fuck was that possible did she fly there?

Chapter Thirteen

DANITY

I had that nigga Dee's phone tapped ever since my brother had told me that he was seeming suspect. I didn't like him or his nasty ass sister. I was not going to play about my brother. I had heard a couple of Dee's conversations talking shit about my brother. He was saying that Maurice thought he was the man and if he knew who was the connect then Maurice wouldn't be the man, anymore he would. He had me fucked up if he thought that I was going to let anything happen to my brother. I had that shit tatted on my damn hand for a reason. I am my brother's keeper. There wasn't no if, ands, or buts about it. I was already by the hood just because I like the little store where they sold them bomb ass nachos. My Mom had called me and told me about Auntie Mya being diagnosed with brain cancer and it had fucked me up a bit. I noticed since then Tre was trying to get a bit closer to me. He asked me on a date I didn't know what the fuck was wrong with him. I am not gone lie after I came back from Miami I did slip up and have sex with him. I had just made it back home from the airport. I saw him sitting in front of my door. I didn't know how the fuck he was able to get in my building, but he needed to stop. What if I was with Tip or Julian what the fuck would they think? "Hey Tre" I dryly stated as I went to open my door. He walked behind me "did your mother tell you?" I could hear the tears in his voice. "Yeah," I said as I headed upstairs to my room. He followed me. I didn't stop him for some reason I wanted him to see me naked. I started taking off my clothes right in front of him. I stripped naked and then I turned around to see if he was looking and he was. I walked past him into the bathroom. I turned the steamy hot shower on and stepped in. He was getting undressed. No words needed to be said as he licked on my nipples and kissed my stomach. I wanted him and he wanted me. I knew it was wrong and he knew it was wrong, but it felt good for right now. I lifted my leg up so that he could slide his dick inside my vagina. I was wet and my walls hugged his dick like a glove. "Damn Dan you feel so good" he moaned. I didn't even say anything I just let out a moan. It was feeling good and I was concentrating on cumming. He rammed his dick inside me, and I rotated my hips just right for him. I could tell that he was in love with me. With every stroke but I didn't feel the same way. I felt hate for him, yet the sex was good. I hated Uncle Tre for turning me into a cold-blooded killer, I hated him for fucking me and committing adultery. After he came, I cursed his ass out "get your filthy ass out my house!" I screamed. He looked at me like I was crazy and the he laughed. I could feel the tears streaming down my face and I wanted it to go away. Damn he got to me. He got dressed and I heard the door slam I stood in the bathroom feeling stupid. I was cold and those damn tears just kept coming down my face. I saw Dee pull up and he parked on the corner. There was this little nigga who looked to be around seventeen who got out of the car. They were laughing and the little dude went to hide behind the house. Oh yeah, this nigga was trying to set my brother up. I made sure to make a u turn so that I didn't drive past Dee. I went around the corner so that I could get to the house where no one would see me. I went through the back and I slowly crept. I saw the nigga with his back up against the wall and I could tell he was waiting for Dee to give him the signal. Maurice hadn't made it yet and I was about to talk to this nigga until he did. "Excuse me" I said in a sexy voice. I startled his dumb ass I could tell he was scared to even kill. "What up ma what you doing back here?" He tried to conceal the gun. I looked over in Dee's direction and I saw that Maurice had pulled up. "Look lil mama you need to get the fuck out of here because shit is about to get real." He turned to point his gun. I pulled the gun from my back and shot him in the back of his head. He was stupid. I had a silencer. I crouched down behind some bushes. I didn't want to show myself just of yet. I heard Reese talking. "So, nigga you been blowing me up so what the fuck is going on?" Reese asked Dee. "Man, I need my supply." Dee tried to buff up at Reese. "Nigga didn't I say you was acting suspect go find you another plug nigga cause mine not fucking with you." I could tell Dee was getting nervous because his nigga had not let off any rounds and he wouldn't because I had killed him. Although I was behind the bushes, I could see that Dee getting nervous. He kept looking in the direction that his mans was supposed to come out at. He was itching to do something I could sense it, I jumped up out the bushes. "Hold the fuck up nigga!" I raised my pistol. This situation was fucked up because it was the middle of daylight and I was not trying to get caught. Yes, half these damn houses were abandoned but it was a chance that somebody was inside them. "Danity what the fuck you doing here?" Dee was shook. "I am my brother's keeper" I replied as I let off four rounds to his body. Dee's body shook as the bullets filled his chest. He hit the ground hard. "Dan! Not in broad daylight!" Reese was yelling at me, but I didn't give a fuck. "Get the fuck out of here!" He yelled. I started running towards my car. That was stupid and I should have been smart about it. Fuck it the deed was done.

Chapter Fourteen
MAURICE

Danity was a fucking hothead! Damn the girl was crazy I had to laugh. That nigga Dee had really been trying to set me up, fuck ass nigga. We had been homeboys for a minute and that is how he repay me. I called Pops to let him know what had happened. If anyone was watching or anything then we were surely fucked. She didn't have to shoot him in broad daylight, but it was over now. Pops said that he would handle everything I was grateful that he said that. Damn! With technology and shit these days you just had to be careful. Usually Danity was careful I didn't know what the fuck that was about, but I was going to get to the bottom of it. I made my way to her apartment I was going to use my key, but I decided to knock instead. I heard some shouting coming from inside and I recognized Danity's voice. I inserted my key and let myself in. When I walked in the nigga Julian had my sister hemmed up against her wall. The nigga had me fucked up. Danity still had on her clothes from the shooting so I knew that he had been waiting on her. I didn't know the nigga Julian too well, but I knew that he was a certified killer. Although I had never killed before I knew I would over my sister. "Let her go nigga!" I yelled. He turned around and he must not had known I had entered. He didn't look shocked or scared he looked crazy. The scowl on his face was menacing and I saw death before my eyes. He threw Danity across the room and I knew he was trying to be funny because I had told him to let her go. "What the fuck you gone do nigga?" He asked stepping closer to me. Danity ran towards Julian and he didn't even look back as he reached and grabbed her by her neck. I had secured my pistol and put it up ready to aim and fire. Before I could a shot rang out. I ducked as I looked in search of who had let off a shot. The bullet pierced through Julian's temple, his body fell to the ground lifeless. Julian released Danity and she fell to the floor coughing for to breath. Tre ran to her and grabbed her up. She was coughing. She was trying to talk I ran to get her some water out of the fridge. "We gotta get out of here. Dan, I know you just moved here but you gone have to move." Tre grabbed his phone out of his pocket and started making calls. Danity drank the water fast as hell. When she caught her breath, she began to talk low only for me to hear "don't ever do that Malcolm." She never used my real name unless she was serious or scared. I was confused what had I done? "What are you talking about?" "Don't ever kill that is something you should never do. It's not easy to live with yourself once you do it." The look in her eyes was that of a scared little girl. I didn't say anything as I hugged my sister. She was trying to protect me when I was the one who was supposed to be protecting her. She was my everything. I know that day we saw that officer get killed in front of us had affected each of us in a different way. I had appreciated life and wanted to move in silence. Danity she moved in silence, but she had a craving for killing. The first time she told me she had killed that guy that was trying to kill Uncle Tre I knew she had lost her soul. Her hazel brown eyes were lifeless as she told me about it. I hugged her and I will never forget what she whispered in my ear as she cried. "I am crying because I loved it. The feeling of killing brought me so much joy." That is what my little sister told me at the age of fourteen. I didn't know what to say so I just held her tighter. I knew about the nightmares she endured. I knew about the battle of whether what she was doing is right or wrong. It was morally wrong, yet it felt right to her. Killing for her was like a drug. I knew she had to get it from somewhere. It wasn't just that cop being killed it was more to it, the reason she craved death. Our father was dead, and I remember memories of him beating on my Mother. I really did not know if he was a killer, I needed to ask my Mom a couple of questions. I mean she was a sweet lady, but I always wanted to ask her what happened to our stepdad Rashad. When she came back, she came with Crenshaw and she never spoke about him again. So that led me to believe she was hiding something. Tre got off the phone "what the fuck was that about Danity?" "He came at me talking about he knows that I am cheating on him." Danity said with her head down. "Juelz, you was fucking Juelz?" Tre was shaking his head. "Girl that nigga is a fucking ruthless killer how long has that shit been going on?" "It doesn't even matter" I interrupted him. The nigga was asking my sister too much shit. Fuck that it doesn't matter the nigga shouldn't have come at her like that. Uncle Tre looked at me like he wanted to murder me. Yeah nigga I loved you, but I no longer had respect for the hoe ass nigga. He was fucking my little sister too. "Nigga need to worry about they wife and shit." I made sure to say. "The fuck you saying boy!" He walked up on me, I jumped up. "Y'all calm down!" Danity jumped in the middle of us. "Man, the clean-up crew will be here in like five minutes Dan to clean this shit up. Try to keep your damn pussy in them clothes so shit like this won't happen." Tre said as he walked out of her loft. "Fuck that pussy!" I made sure to say loud enough for him to hear. "You can stay with me until you find someplace else." Dani ty shook her head and she headed to the back to take a shower. Two big ass niggas came to the door and I knew they must have been the cleanup crew. For Tre to be a seasoned killer the nigga was sloppy. He didn't even use a silencer I was surprised that no one had called the cops yet. I went in the back to Danity's room while those niggas cleaned the body up. This shit was too much I needed for my little sister to stop livi ng t his lifestyle because this shit was getting out of hand.

Chapter Fifteen
DANITY

I was mad as fuck that Julian had pulled that shit. Like he knew that we were not exclusive, so I felt that whole situation at the house was a set up but a set up for what? I had been at Maurice's house for a week now and Uncle Tre was steady calling me. It was more to this situation and I was trying to figure it out. After killing Dee I took the long route home. Nothing seemed out of place as I walked through the hallways. I was not on point because I did not even see Julian's car in my parking garage. I unlocked my door, and everything seemed fine until I got all the way inside and found Julian going through my kitchen cabinets. "What the fuck Ju! What you doing looking in my damn cabinets?" I asked him. He didn't respond right away. He looked around as he tried to search for words. "Bitch you fucking somebody else." He rushed me before I could respond. He grabbed me into the air. I was struggling to breath when Maurice saved my ass. That was all that I had gotten from Julian because Tre killed him. That was another thing that was bothering me. How the hell did Uncle Tre just show up to save the day? Like is the nigga following me or what? Yeah, this shit was not adding up I wanted answers, but I had to sit and think on the situation. Maurice came home later that night about seven. My brother was a true ass hustler for real. He was moving so much damn weed, and no one even knew that shit was brilliant. The alias he was using was Cobra and muthafuckas thought he was the middleman that shit was smart. I know that he was working hard trying to make money. I just didn't know the drive behind his hustle everybody worked to get somewhere. I mean was this nigga trying to run the streets or was he just trying to make a quick come up. I didn't know what it was. For example, I was working to change my identity and move far the fuck away. Of course, I would let my mother and brother know where I was, but I just wanted to run away. I had a quarter of a million saved and I was just sitting on it. I had wanted to make the move once I turned eighteen, but shit started happening and it's just not that easy to pull away from this business. As soon as Maurice came home, we were about to sit down and talk when his phone started ringing. "Wait, slow down" I could see the worry lines in his face, and I was ready to kill. "I am on my way." "What up bro?" I jumped up ready to move. He laughed "Damn Dan you trained to go. That was just my little shorty she said somebody broke into her daycare." "What your little shorty? No more Chastity? Well I guess not after that shit with Dee. I am going I want to meet her." I grabbed my jacket. We pulled up to the building. There was a police car outside, and that shit spooked me. I hated the cops especially because I worked for one. I knew exactly how dirty they could be. We walked in and there was a girl with blonde dreads crying. That must be her. The cops were acting like she had broken into her own shit. The line of questioning they were asking her was rude and unnecessary. There was shit everywhere. You could tell she had good taste though. "So ma'am what the suspect look like?" One of the officers asked. "I don't know he had on a mask I keep telling you." She cried into her hands. "Ma'am what are you doing here after hours?" I knew that voice. I walked closer and it was him. His white ass was crooked as they came. He had done a couple of jobs with me too. "Andrew stop asking her so much shit!" I screamed to get his attention. "Dollface?" He smiled at me. I rolled my eyes at Andrew. He was a dirty son of a bitch, but he got the job done. "Yeah it's me. Why the hell you asking, this girl so many questions?" I walked closer and Maurice was hugging on her. She was cute as hell and I must admit my brother had good taste. All of Andrew's professionalism went out the window "shit all this sound suspect. Some muthafucka just coming in here throwing shit around and he didn't even rape her or anything?" "Aye muthafucka!" Maurice yelled. I was smiling that was Andrew for you straight forward. "Man, I am just saying" his green eyes stared into my brown eyes and I knew what he was thinking about. I turned away. "Aye you got everything you need my man?" Maurice walked over and pulled me towards him. He saw the lustful look in Andrew's eyes. "Yeah my man," Andrew headed out, but he turned towards me. "Dollface I miss you." I already knew that. I didn't respond he took it for what it was and exited the building. Maurice muffed me on the side of my head. "Damn girl how many niggas have you been fucking?" "Fuck you nigga!" I rolled my eyes and stomped out of the building. I got into Maurice's car I didn't have time to go back and forth with him. The nerve of him to embarrass me in front of that girl like that. It wasn't long before he came out with her by his side. She climbed in the back and I rolled my eyes. He reached over and kissed my cheek. "I am sorry honey." My big brother apologized. I rolled my eyes "don't get mad at me because I pull these niggas from left to right." He sped off. I turned around towards the blonde dread head. "I am Maurice's little sister Danity and to forewarn you he is pure asshole." I turned back around. Hell yeah, I was throwing salt in his game. "Danity don't be saying that shit. She already giving me a hard time saying she like girls." Maurice pouted. I looked back at her. She was way to pretty to be bumping pussies. "Keep the lie alive honey." She laughed. She knew what I meant. I couldn't believe that she was gay. When we made it to her house Maurice walked her to her door like the gentlemen he is. He had pissed me off, but I could tell he was feeling her. So, I did what any sister would have done I d rove off on his ass. I saw them looking staring as I sped away in his car. I needed some time to myself anyways.

Chapter Sixteen

IMANI

I could not believe that Maurice's little sister had sped off in his car. The shit was comical to say the least. I was standing there laughing and I could tell he was pissed because his face turned red. He started calling her back to back but that girl was not answering. He was cute and the way that his gray eyes sparkled even in the dark was sexy to me. "Come on boy she is not coming back no time soon and I am cold." I ushered him into my place. He sat down on the couch and made himself at home by grabbing the remote control. Damn I was starting to think that they had set me up. Then I had to think he was just talking shit to her so I could see why she was mad. I called Shanita's ass to let her know that I was at home. I had let the bitch use my van. She left and then I was robbed at the daycare. I called her before I called Maurice and she still had not called me back. Her phone rang and she answered "what up Mani?" "The fuck you mean Nita! You asked me to use my damn van two hours ago and left me at the daycare and I got robbed!" "Damn baby I didn't know where you at? You called the cops?" She asked all the questions she should have asked an hour ago, had she answered her phone. "Fuck all that bring me my shit I am at home!" I yelled into the phone and hung it back up on the charger. She knows she saw I was calling from my house number. I walked back into the living room where Maurice fine ass was sitting. I had never been with a man before. My older sister Icyss was married with three kids but I don't know men never intrigued me until I met Maurice. I sat next to him and got nervous I needed a drink. I went and got the bottle of Grey Goose to satisfy me. "Damn Imani you ready to turn up with a nigga huh? It has been a long day my crazy ass sister done just dumped me on your ass." I looked at him and didn't respond I took a shot to the head. Damn he was so sexy the way he talked was just turning me on. I had never felt like this. I grabbed the glass and poured another shot and swallowed it. I was not much of a drinker, but I knew that if I had three more shots, I was liable to fuck Maurice right here and right now. Fuck it. "Damn girl slow down," he grabbed the bottle from my hand after I had poured my fourth shot. He brushed his hand against my hand and the electricity sent nervous giggles through my body. I was laughing and didn't even care that he saw that I was drunk. I heard the knock on the door and knew that it was Shanita's bitch ass. I went to the door and I saw Maurice reach for his pistol. "Chill it ain't nobody but my punk ass ex." I said slurring my words. I know she heard me because I purposely said it while opening the door. There she stood 5'4 and two hundred and fifty pounds of her. I did not know what the fuck I was thinking. She was my first and my only and I loved her. She was a cheater and she didn't have shit. She didn't have a job, she lived with her Mom, smoked weed all day and thought she was a man what the fuck was I thinking? "Man shut the fuck up" she whined as she entered the apartment. She looked at Maurice and he looked at her "what the fuck is this Mani?" I snatched my car keys out of her hand. "I don't have to explain shit to you we not together." I was drunk but I knew what I was talking about. "Get the fuck out!" She didn't even resist she just left. After I locked my door I went back and sat next to Maurice and he looked at me and started cracking up. I did not see what the fuck was so funny. "What the fuck is so funny!" I said a little bit too loud for myself. "That's what you like Imani?" He asked through laughter. "Oh, you think the shit funny. You get your ass out too." I started swinging on him. He grabbed my arms and pinned me up against the couch. I was laying down and he was on top of me "Aye girl ain't none of that shit I am a real man." "I know" I lustfully said and kissed his lips. I tell you I ain't never kissed a man before and it was just something about the way his mustache rubbed against my lip. I loved it, it was so masculine and not feminine like what I was used to. He kept kissing me and he allowed me to suck on his tongue. He grabbed the buttons on my pants and undid them. Yess! I was thinking take these muthafuckas off! He pulled my pants down and removed my panties. I was staring at him as I supported myself on my elbows. "You want me to lick this pussy or you want to feel me?" He asked me. Damn he was so fine I just wanted to fuck. "Let's go to the bedroom." I told him. I led him into my bedroom, and he laid me on the bed. I opened my legs up for him and he undressed for me. All those damn abs and all that damn body he was going to give me a night to remember I just knew it. He released that big ass dick from his boxers and my eyes widened. He smirked he was going to give me the business. My anticipation was building up and I wanted it so bad. He crawled on the bed. "Open your legs" he demanded, and I obliged. He was about to penetrate me when we heard a car honking. Damn it, it was his sister! He jumped up and looked out the window. "DAMN!" I knew he was mad, but I was madder than him. "I am sorry baby but my damn sister back. I know we are going.." his phone started ringing and he answered. "Danity calm the hell down. I am about to come out right now. I am coming down right now." He was putting on his clothes fast as he hung up the phone. "I am so sorry, but some shit is going down I will holla at you alright." I had jumped up by this time and was had thrown on my robe. "Okay just call me if you need me." I said back. To say I was pissed would be an understatement. I wanted that dick so bad I could taste it. Damn another day. I locked my door and went back to bed. I checked my phone and saw ten messages from Shanita. All she was talking about was how I was now fucking with a man. So, the fuck what I didn't need that shit. I needed a real man and I was tired of bumping pussies. I needed to get penetrated and not by no damn tongue. As soon as I sorted shit out at the daycare tomorrow Maurice was going to be all mine I could not wait.

Chapter Seventeen

MYA

The news of being terminally ill was devastating. I had beaten this disease before and I thought that it was gone. Hearing the news that I needed to get comfortable to die was indescribable. Nothing could take my pain away that I knew when I was going to die. I thought that dying was the worse thing that could happen to me. It was like the devil was playing a trick on me. Although, preparing for death was difficult learning that the little girl I raised was fucking my husband was worst. I had mistakenly taken Tre's phone on my way to the grocery store. I needed to get out of the house. He was sound asleep as I crept out the house. I was finishing up shopping when a text message came through the phone. Danity 'Damn Julian was out of order but so are we Tre. This shit has to end no more fucking! Okay this shit should just be business.' I had to reread the message because the name at the top just could not be who I thought it was, but it was it was A'Deena better known as Danity. After their mother came back, I remained in their lives. I just did not understand why she would betray me like this. I wondered did her mother know what was going on. Then, she said business. What kind of business was he doing with an 18-year-old girl? As I shattered the phone on the pavement as I exited the store, it didn't stop my heart from breaking. The entire ride home I held on to my emotions. I was numb, I was dying, and my husband was cheating with my best friend's daughter. When I got back home Tre was smiling as I entered the front door. I only had one bag in my hand. He grabbed the bag as he asked me about his phone. "Damn babe you know where my phone at?" He questioned. "In a million pieces." I said walking pat him. "What do you mean?" He asked as he followed behind me. I turned around with rage in my eyes and I know he could see it "since you want to fuck on Danity I broke your phone! Just like you broke my heart deal with it." I turned back around and did not say anything. He sat the bag on the kitchen table and walked out. I could hear him moving around upstairs. Then he came running down the stairs and out the door. The tears escaped my eyes and I didn't want them too. To be crying over a man that would be crazy at this point in my life. I was dying and there was nothing I could do about it. I was mad because I wanted to know more, and I needed to know more. I was going to cook but it just wasn't in me anymore I needed to speak with the only one who held the answers to my questions. I raced out the house full force. I needed answers and I needed them now. As soon as I pulled up at her house, I was happy that I saw her Bentley truck. I got out of my car and started banging on the door. I was so hot and heated that I felt like I was going to fall out any moment. Crenshaw opened the door. He was handsome as ever and I was mad because I figured he knew too. I pushed him out my way. "Ay girl what's your problem?" He probed. I stood in the middle of their living room with the tall ceiling. "Aniya! Aniya! Aniya!" I started screaming loud as I could. Crenshaw ran into the room. "What the hell Mya?" I didn't get a chance to answer him because Aniya walked into the room. "Mya what is the matter?" She asked looking at me. She was beautiful as usual with her short hair and pouty big lips. She was remarkably cute and right now I was mad and didn't want to think about how she was my best friend. "Your daughter is fucking my husband." I was still shocked, but the look that Aniya gave me I knew that she knew. "You knew didn't you?" "Look Mya just sit down and let's talk." She said as she guided me to the couch. Crenshaw was still hovering over us. I didn't give a damn because I know he knew what was going on too. "Look Mya I know she had sex with Tre. I have been waiting for her to talk to me about it, but she still haven't. I didn't want to hurt you because I didn't know what was going on." I started crying "you not to blame Niya it is their fault." My heart was broken as I sat in sorrow. "I feel fucked up Mya I really do." Niya hugged me, her embraced felt so good and it made me break down more. I was crying so hard and fast that I just knew any moment my damn head was going to explode. To find out you have maybe a month to live and then that your husband is cheating this was just too much for me. Not only was he cheating he was cheating with someone I thought of as a daughter. This shit hurt more than I wanted it too. Danity had been estranged from me since she was about fourteen and she started clinging onto Tre more. I chalked it up as a teenager thing and didn't think more of it. Now I was sitting here beating myself up because I should have known or suspected. Was he molesting this young girl back then? Danity had just turned eighteen so if he was having sex with her before that he was a molester. She was not who I should have been mad at he was. He was a married man who had used this young girl. That was how I looked at it and that was how the world should view it. Tre was a sad muthafucka and I hated him. When I got back home Tre was there sitting in the living room as if nothing had happened. I walked up to him and slapped his face. He looked up at me and I didn't see the Tre I had married I saw a monster. He smiled as he got up off the couch. "You done!" He bellowed. I was scared for a minute but then I remembered something. I was not in the wrong, I was the one who was dying! Fuck him and the bullshit that came with him. "Hell naw muthafucka! You want to do something to me?" He grabbed my arm I could see the evil in his eyes then he softened up. "Calm down Mya I know you mad but you gotta hear me out." I calmed myself down and sat next to my husband. Although I was livid with him, I still loved him. Love just didn't go away in a couple of hours. "Danity came on to me. It was after her birthday when you and I was having problems. She told me to come over because she was scared because she thought she was being followed. I as an Uncle did as I was told and went to make sure she was alright. She came to the door in her robe and seduced me that was just that one time nothing else." He had tears in his eyes. Damn my man was seduced by my God daughter. I was mad at him it wasn't his fault it was her fault. "When I tried to tell Amber about the shit, she brushed me off." He said as he grabbed me and held me tight.

I held onto my husband as he cried on my shoulder. This man was afraid to lose me. I loved him and even if I died that bitch Danity was not going to have him. You could bet on that.

"Maurice where the fuck is your sister? I am tired of her hiding out." I was at my son's house and I knew that my daughter was there. Maurice told me everything, so I knew she was here at his home. Maurice looked at me like I had lost my mind. "Ma don't come over here starting stuff." I pushed his high yella ass out the way "boy shut the fuck up I am your Mother!" When I walked in the living room there, she was my beloved daughter. Danity was beautiful. She had inherited my hazel brown eyes. She had long, curly hair that fell to the middle of her back, and people swore she was half white, but she wasn't. Her petite frame was covered in a Pink outfit. She smiled when she saw me, but she knew what was up. Maurice made his way to the living room. "Don't fucking smile at me you been hiding long enough." I sat next to her. Her smiled was still there but you could tell it was forced. "Ma calm down" Maurice piped in. Ugh the damn boy pissed me off sometimes because he looked so much like his Daddy. If my son had not had such a good personality, I would have thought Hakeem had come back alive in my baby. I rolled my eyes at him and turned my attention back on Danity "so...care to explain?" "Ma it is not even like that Uncle Tre came on to me. It happened and it was a big mistake." I loved the sound of my daughter's voice. Even when I was mad at her she could simmer me down with her voice. It was quiet and reserved. "Look I know things happen, but Mya knows. I don't know how but she knows." "Damn" Maurice said, and I looked at him like he was crazy. "Sorry ma." "I don't know what to say Ma I mean I didn't want to hurt Auntie Mya and I really do love her. I couldn't even speak to y'all and tell y'all what had happened Ma I am really embarrassed and feel ashamed." I grabbed my daughter and hugged her "I know baby and I love Mya too, but you my baby. Fuck that I will do anything to protect y'all and you know that." I meant every word. I had done so much shit in the past that I knew that if it came to it, I would kill Tre and Mya if they ever threatened my children's life. I didn't know why but something was telling me it might come to that. I had written Mya letters years ago when she had my children. I had kind of given her a look into my life but for some reason I never told her about how I had taken lives. I knew that she was not to be trusted. She was my best friend and I loved her but shit right now was one of those times when I was happy that I kept shit to myself. She was not aware of the damage that I could do and because of that if her or her husband came at my daughter wrong then I was going to unleash Aniya. Yeah, I am sweet, soft spoken, gorgeous, and could cook a three-course meal, but with them guns I am deadly. I do not play about my seeds. "Okay it is alright I just wish you would have come to me with what happened. Did he ever do anything to you when you were younger?" "No ma'am" she responded a little too quickly for me. I made my way back to my house where my husband Crenshaw was waiting for me. He was my everything after being in som e fuc ked u p relationships, I really appreciated him. He was at the computer looking at some information about our businesses. He had turned from a criminal to a damn businessman and I loved it. I had tried to turn my ex-husband into a businessman but no he wanted to run the streets and because of that it cost him his life. "Hey baby" I walked up and kissed him. "Hey baby did you talk to Dan?" Crenshaw was concerned. "Yes" I sat on his lap. "Tre came on to her" he didn't say anything. I looked at him. "What do you think baby?" "You want me to be honest?" He asked me. "Yes bae." I needed his advice on this one. "Okay I think they came on to each other. I think that they have gotten close over the years. They both have gotten feelings for each other beyond the Uncle and niece relationship." I nodded my head. Crenshaw maybe right, but I had asked Danity and I wanted her to be honest. I think she put the blame on him so that she wouldn't look bad. I knew the lifestyle Tre had introduced my daughter too and to be honest I didn't like his ass. Who leads a child to be a killer it wasn't right. I felt the vibration from my phone. I opened it up to a long text from Mya. Mya 'your daughter is a hoe and she seduced my husband with her nasty pussy. I hope she know that I will not take this disrespect lying down. We were friends but now we are not. It is because of your slut of a daughter. She will never have my husband NEVER! Fuck you and your kids! I have only a limited time to live and I would appreciate if you and your kids would stay away from my husband and I.' She had officially lost her mind. If she didn't have a death sentence, then me being the type of bitch I was would have ended her. I let Crenshaw read the text and he started laughing the shit was not funny at all to me. "Stop laughing!" I shouted. "Dang baby you have to admit it is funny I know you don't think Mya wrote this shit. This has Tre all over it. He did this shit. I have known him for a long time. This shit doesn't even sound like Mya" I had to agree with my husband he was right that shit was not like Mya to say no shit like that. I put my phone back in my pocket and forgot all about that bullshit I had bigger fish to fry. "Babe I will be back?" I headed out the door. "Quita?" "Yep," I said as I headed to my next destination. I told Chiquita that I would meet her in the food court at the mall. I was not scared of her, but I knew she didn't like me. Chiquita was my baby's daddy Hakeem sister. The bitch was in jail for trying to kill me and my kids. She had gotten out along with his other baby mama Cedes. I had not heard from Cedes but her sons were always bringing her up. I didn't know how the fuck Cedes got out. I had a funny feeling about her and whenever the bitch reappeared, I was going to bring the heat to her ass too. I saw Quita walking up and I knew it was her. She had gotten a bit smaller but she was still big. I waved her over and she smiled like she had not been calling me talking shit. She sat down with me. "Hey Niya." She faked a smile. "No formalities Quita I am tired of you calling me." I cut right to the chase this hoe had tried to kill me wasn't no being nice shit. She had come all the way to California I know the bitch had beef. She rolled her eyes "Well since you said it like that bitch, I need my money." Quita was not longer the beauty that she had been before. Yes, she was always a big girl, but prison had been hard on her. She had gray hairs and the wrinkles around her eyes told me she was tired. "Your money is spent next question?" I didn't bat an eye. "What the fuck you mean?" She got upset. "Quita I do not owe you shit I inherited all of Hakeem's business. You still on this dumb shit bitch you tried to kill me. Whatever money you had you obviously spent it because you sitting in front of me asking for my money." "I ain't trying to hear that shit I helped him start them companies now you tell me I don't get shit!" She was loud and a couple of people looked at us. I was not moved. "Bitch you killed nice people who took you in FUCK YOU! Matter of fact..." I tossed her a grand. "Bitch you better use that money wisely" I got up and headed out the door. I could hear her shouting out threats to me, but I was unfazed fuck her. All the shit I had to put up with she had me fucked up. I made my way to my car and blew out air. I was ready to kill if I had too. I knew this was not my last time hearing from Chiquita, but right now she was going to have to come harder. When she did, I was going to be ready I had several bullets with her name on them. I had allowed her to know my location for a reason.

Chapter Nineteen
TRE

Way too much shit was going on. Mya was dying and then she found out about Danity. Man, that shit fucked me up. I shot Amber that text to just make sure she didn't reach out to Mya anymore. I wanted her die with just me and her and no one else around. I wanted Danity she had been acting funny ever since that shit with Julian. Speaking of Julian, I had to meet up with his crazy ass. Yeah, I know I know I shot him. Nah that nigga is one of the best. That shit was all a set-up he was not supposed to get caught by Dani ty. He was stupid and so when I came, I pretended to shoot him he knew the routine. He was good at playing dead. We met up on the other side of town. I had direct orders to find out who the fuck The Plug was, and I had not found out shit. All the drug dealers were saying that they got their products from a middleman. When I found out who the middleman was I was shocked, Maurice my nephew. I didn't even know he was in the street life I considered him a square. We all thought he was going to school to be a damn chemist but from what I was hearing out on the streets he was a fucking hustler. I needed to get more information about it. I knew the way shit was playing out that I was not his favorite guy so he would get suspicious if I asked him. It was time to put Julian on the case. The easiest way to get information was from Danity. I knew she was staying at the niggas house. Julian was sitting at the table in my office looking sad and shit. He was fucked up behind the fact that I was fucking Danity too. I was mad as fuck when I found out she was fucking Julian. I wanted to kill that nigga right now, but I had more important shit to do like get this assignment done then he was a dead man. "What up?" I greeted Julian. "You tell me nigga so you been fucking Danity too?" He got up out his seat. You could see the heat coming from his face and I got a bit scared. He was a big man and I knew the damage that he could do but I was a bad muthafucka too. "Pipe down nigga she ain't shit but a piece of ass. So, I got an assignment for you." "I want out Tre." Julian said his eyes were low and cold. I couldn't believe this nigga was doing this shit right now. Like what the fuck was he on. He knew the only way out was through a body bag unless... I turned around and the barrel of the gun was staring me right in my face. "Julian for real?" I wasn't scared of dying but right now was not the time, my wife was dying. "Yes, for real Tre I can't do it anymore." I wasn't really paying him anymore I was looking at the brown skinned beauty that he had decided to determine my faith with. She was beautiful and she had cocoa brown skin. She had a curly weave in hair that fit her perfectly. I couldn't see her body, but I knew it was gorgeous too. I turned my attention back to Julian. This bitch didn't look like she had heart enough to kill me. "Nigga what is the problem? I came here to talk business." I moved away from the gun. She wasn't about shit, so I didn't give a fuck I knew she was all talk and no guts. Julian looked at her crazy. Since I moved, she was supposed to let off rounds into my body, she didn't. I knew she was bluffing. I knew a killer when I saw one and she was no damn killer. Her hands were shaking when she held the gun to my face. I sat down and grabbed my gun from under my chair. I quickly pulled it from the chair and shot right in between her eyes. Her body hit the floor with a loud thump. "Nigga what were you thinking having a weak ass bitch pull a gun on me!" I growled. Julian started laughing. He was laughing so hard it caused me to laugh. He made it to the chair in front of my desk. "Okay nigga she said she wanted to be down man I was testing her out." "Man fuck her nigga I need you to get on this assignment and I need you to follow my nephew Maurice. I been on this assignment to stop the fucking plug that has been flooding the streets and not paying taxes. Well word on the street is that he is the middleman that means he know who the plug is. I need that information without him know I am looking for it. My guess is that it is some Mexicans or some niggas from L.A. Julian understood what needed to be done and he set out on his assignment. I on the other hand dialed Danity's number. When it gave me, this number has been changed message I instantly got pissed. Where the fuck was this bitch at? She getting on my nerves. I got up and stormed out of my office. When I made it to my car, I saw that my wife was calling. I did not feel like hearing that depressing, woah is me shit, so I pressed ignore. I pulled up to the gym that I knew Danity went to and I read my watch yup she was due to be here any minute. I saw her car pull up and I hopped right out. She was looking good with her yoga pants on. She had her long curly hair hanging. "Danity!" I called after her. She knew it was me and she kept walking. I wanted to whoop this bitch ass right now. I ran up on her and grabbed her arm she didn't even flinch. "What Uncle Tre?" She asked matter of factly. "Oh, it's Uncle Tre now huh?" "It been Uncle Tre what do you want?" She rolled her eyes. "Why the fuck you change your number?" I questioned her. "Cause I don't want you to call me." She stated arrogantly. "What the fuck you mean you don't want me to call you? Bitch you work for me." She slapped me as soon as she heard the bitch word. I didn't say anything I knew how she was. "Look Danity we have assignments to do." "Okay, I understand that, and I am all about my bread. But nigga you texting me shit about how you want to fuck." "Shit I do but business first. I need some muthafuckas to disappear that is first then I will worry about fucking your little brains out." She sucked her teeth "nigga please you will not be hitting this again." "Oh really" I grabbed her face and kissed her. I could feel her body melt. Once I let her go, she looked disgusted. "Nigga please like I said no more pussy for you. I will be calling you for an assignment and that is it Uncle Tre!" She said a bit loudly. I saw people staring at us in disgust. She did that shit on purpose she was an ignorant little bitch. She walked into the gym and I was satisfied as soon as she called me. I was going to make that pussy purr and she was not going to want to stop fucking me. My wife was dying and Danity was going to be my runner up. I was a man who had done many things but living without a woman was not something that I could handle. No one knew this but I had been married before. I had killed my first wife a week before I had met Mya. She was a beautiful woman her name was Ramesha. The bitch was a straight hood rat. We had gotten married at a young age. I loved Ramesha and she introduced me to this game of killing. Ramesha was fine black as night with even darker eyes. Her hair was short like a boy haircut, but she was a beauty. I loved everything about the woman. One day after we were married, she told me to take her to Wendy's she was acting like she was in a hurry. I told her to come on. At the time I was in school for criminal justice. Ramesha wasn't doing shit from what I knew she was just a hoodrat trying to snag a good nigga. I was that nigga. We pulled up to the Wendy's and there was a guy sitting in his BMW. Mesha called someone on her phone and started saying his license plate number. I'm looking at the bitch like she crazy. She hangs up and I get to asking her what the fuck was that about. She tells me to pull next to him on her side. I do as I am told but I am hot at this moment. She raises down her window and open fire into the car. I was in disbelief I even screamed like a little bitch. "Drive Tre" she said very calmly. I was scared as shit and I needed to calm myself down. I pulled down a few blocks and started yelling at her ass. "Just calm down," she pulled out a bunch of money from her purse. She started counting it was ten thousand dollars all in one hundred-dollar bills. "Tre this is what I do for a living I don't need to work because I got us. Don't be scared." She kissed my lips. "You a fucking hired killer?" I questioned. "Yeah." I didn't join the club right away though. I met her boss which is my boss now and I got welcomed into the family. They taught me everything and Ramesha was one of the best. That is why when it was her time to go it was up to me to do the deed. It was way easier than I had thought because when it came time to kill Mesha I found out so much shit while following her. That bitch was fucking everybody. She was fucking some police officers, dope boys, that is why her time had run out. I didn't know why they really wanted her dead. Once I found out all that information the reason didn't matter because, now I had my own reason. I met Crenshaw in the mix of forming my own team before Ramesha was killed. He didn't know I was married before because he didn't stay around me for a long time. He was a hustler and I understood that, that is why I let him go. Now that I thought about it, it was possible that he might be the plug. Crenshaw was from Cali and it just made me think the guy that I had sacrificed was now possibly a target. If so, he was going to have to be dealt with but until I gathered enough information I was going to stand back and let all the information colle ct. No assumptions and no fuck ups. That was the rules.

Chapter Twenty

MYA

The pain I was feeling was excruciating. My head felt like it was going to explode. I had not talked to Aniya in a while and I did not understand. I wanted my friend back. One day I wanted her and the next day I didn't. I know it was the tumor and my head that was driving me crazy. I tried calling Tre, but the pain was horrible to the point if I even opened my eyes it was like a drum was beating on my head. I fell to sleep and when I woke up, I was in the hospital. I looked around and saw Aniya. I smiled and tried to talk, but there was a tube down my throat. Aniya was crying as she looked at me. "Don't try to talk honey you had a stroke. It was bad." She explained to me. A stroke? Damn my days on Earth were numbered. I started crying. Aniya tried to calm me but there was no stopping the tears. I heard the monitor going crazy and I was out again. I did not know what was going on and where was my husband. When I woke up again, I saw Tre. He was standing over me crying. His tears were wetting my face. He smiled when he saw my eyes open. "Doctor!" He yelled as he walked out of the room. He came back with a doctor who was looking at me. He did some things to see if I could feel him, but I couldn't. "Yes, she is paralyzed I don't think it is reversible with the state that her body is in. It is best if she just stays in hospice. We will make her last days better." The doctor said. I wanted to scream, and I wanted to go home but I knew that was not going to happen. The doctor was telling Tre that it was time to make my funeral arrangements. He was talking like I was not there. The tears were coming again out of my eyes. I could not believe that this was happening. My sister Monica entered the hospital room and it delighted me. "How is she?" She asked Tre. He started crying "it's all bad Monica. She is dying. She had a stroke I found her in the bed at home. I rushed her to the hospital. They said the tumor has grown she is paralyzed she can't move shit!" He cried. Monica was crying and I was crying too. My death was coming so fast. I did not know what to do. There was nothing I could do but lay here and accept my fate. I drifted off to sleep. When I woke up again my mother was sitting at my bedside. She was beautiful even in her old age. She smiled when she saw me. Her brown eyes sparkled. I loved my mother and I was so pissed I was breaking her heart because I was dying before her. "My precious baby girl I love you so much." My mother cried. I cried with her. My Dad came over to the bed so that I could see him. I looked just like my father. He was still a healthy man. His green eyes were shining, and I loved the way he looked at me with so much love. "I love you muffin." He cried as he kissed my head. Aniya appeared at my bedside. She was in tears and her hair was tied down with a scarf. "I am so sorry for not being a better friend." She cried. She didn't have to say that. She was a good friend to me. Then Danity appeared. She was beautiful. That long curly hair and those eyes she was gorgeous. "I love you Auntie Mya and I appreciate you so much. I would never intentionally do anything to hurt you." I knew what she was trying to say. I had to forgive the young girl. Maurice came into my view. "Auntie man this shit hurts I don't want to see you go. You are like a second Mom." Maurice said he couldn't finish as the tears started falling. He went out the room and a girl with dreadlocks followed him. Tre was the last one to speak "I love you so much. I know I have fucked up, but you were the only person I loved. You are always going to be that one for me." He kissed my cheek. I couldn't speak. "It is time to let her go." The doctors stated. I didn't know why he was saying it was time for me to go? I probably had a couple of more days. Was I going to hospice what was going on? "Why? She is looking at us and she knows what we are saying. Look at the tears coming down her face?" Aniya cried. "She is going to suffer" Tre said. "What the fuck ever. I can't stay." Aniya said as she stormed out of the room Crenshaw was behind her. I didn't know what was going on. I watched as Tre gave the doctor a package. The doctor opened it up and put it in my IV. Tre held my hand as my vital organs started to shut down. I stared him in his eyes, and he looked sad. He looked sad and tired. As my heart stopped my mind was still thinking he looked tired alright, tired of holding on to me.

Chapter Twenty-One
MAURICE

I was hurting bad. Damn not Auntie Mya. I knew she was sick, but it was like this illness took its toll to fast. I was in the hallway crying at the hospital. I don't care it just felt like Tre was doing the shit on purpose. He might have done something to her for all I knew. The tears were falling from my face as my heart was breaking. Imani embraced me and I cried like a baby. My Mother came out of the room into the hallway with Crenshaw. She was crying but when she saw that I was crying she tri ed to fix herself up. She excused Imani and embraced me. Auntie Mya and I were close, and I just could not handle this. "It's okay baby." My mother said into me. I had to get myself together I should be comforting her. I got myself together. "I am okay Ma." I said to her. Danity walked up to us and hugged us. She was also in tears. To see my little sister in tears like that made me want to cry all over again. Danity was strong so to see her cry was making it worse. "I am going to drop Imani off you gone be good sis?" I asked her. She nodded her head yes. She had moved into her new apartment last week. I was worried about her, but she seemed like she would be okay. When we left out of the hospital the sky was cloudy. It hardly ever rained in California and if it did today, I knew why. The angels were going to be crying as they opened the door for another one. Imani rubbed my arm the entire time we rode to her house. My stomach was in knots. My phone was blowing up from Chastity. She had been calling me trying to find her brother. I told her I didn't know where he was and that he owed me some money. My phone rang again, and I guess it annoyed Imani because she grabbed it. "Hello!" She yelled into the phone. I looked over at her like she had lost her mind. "He right here but he is busy stop fucking calling his phone." She hung up the phone and turned it off. I started laughing "damn you mad or nah?" She laughed at me "I ain't mad that shit is just annoying. To keep calling a person's phone like damn they not answering." I turned the corner and parked in her parking lot. I turned off the ignition. "Maurice are you coming in?" "Nah ma I am just gone get something to eat and go home." "Maurice I can cook please don't leave me." She said grabbing my hand. How could I say no to her fine ass? I got out of the car with her. I turned on the television and she went to the kitchen and started making noise. I didn't know what she was about to cook but shit I was ready to eat. I was into the game when she told me the food was done. I got up and sure enough she had hooked it up. Tilapia and spaghetti with a salad it looked good. I sat at the table next to her. Her food was good too. After we were done, she washed the dishes. I watched her clean up. I loved everything about her. I crept up behind her and put my arms around her waist. She looked up at me and smiled. I kissed her. She kissed me back. I turned her around. I stopped kissing her and looked at her. "What Maurice?" "I don't know." I replied cause, I really did not know. She pushed me off her. I grabbed her hand and brought her close to me. I kissed her again. She gave in just like before. I grabbed her under her ass and picked her up. She wrapped her legs around me. I walked her to the bedroom. I had stopped kissing her, but she was kissing me all over my face and neck. I laid her on the bed. I stood up and took off my shirt. I looked at her. She was gorgeous as her dreadlocks framed her face. I positioned myself in between her legs. I kissed her again. She opened her legs wide I knew she was giving me the go head. I stopped and pulled her pants off. She had on some white panties with red hearts. I stood up and took my pants off. She wasn't saying anything as she watched me. When I stepped out of my boxers, she went to take off her panties. She opened her legs so I could see that her cat was shaven. I smiled. I positioned myself between her legs again. I put my dick at her opening. She was wet I tried to push my way into her vagina, but it was tight. "Ummm" she moaned. "Damn I forgot I will be gentle." I said as I kissed her. She returned my kiss. As I took her mind off the pain, I pushed myself into her more. "Ooooooohhh!" she moaned. I knew that it was hurting her, but the shit was feeling good to me. "It's gone start feeling good baby." I told her. I started moving in circles damn this pussy was good as hell. "Ummmm Maurice it hurts" she moaned. "I know baby you want me to stop?" "Noooo" she moaned. I smiled that was right. "That's right you can take this dick this time. It is going to hurt but it will get better." "Ooooh kay" she moaned. I could tell it was starting to get good to her. It was already good to me and as much as I wanted to keep going my nut was ready. I busted in her. She didn't seem to mind since she said it was hurting. I ran her some bath water because I knew she was sore. I told Imani her water was done, and she got up and came to the bathroom. "Get in with me." She told me. I climbed in the tub in the back of her. She laid against me. I hugged her from behind. This felt perfect. After the first time Danity stopped us from having sex I learned something about Imani. She had never felt a real dick inside of her. She only felt vibrators and strap-ons. I told her we could take our time with having sex. We got to know each other very well. I heard snoring and looked down, yeah I had put her to sleep.

Chapter Twenty-Two

DANITY

I could not believe Auntie Mya was dead. We were not on good terms, but I think she forgave me. I went home and started drinking. That bottle of Patron had been calling me. My apartment was not as cute as the other one I had but it would do for now. I got undressed and put on my robe. I could no longer cry it had exhausted me. There was a knock at my door. I assumed it was Maurice since he was the only one who knew where I stayed. I opened the door and was pissed to see Tre standing at my door. I rolled my eyes and tried to close the door, but he stopped it with his foot. I turned and walked away since I knew he was not going to leave. I sat down on my couch. "You was fucking Julian too?" He screamed as he slammed my door. I rolled my eyes he had his nerves his wife had just died.

"Yup and Tip why?" He rushed over to me and slapped me. I looked at him like he was crazy. "You want to be a hoe!" He yelled. "A hoe? Nigga you the hoe! You the one with the dead wife muthafucka! I ain't tied down to nobody so that makes me a free agent. You knew damn well that I was fucking Julian!" I was waiting for another slap, but it never came. He grabbed me and started kissing me "I am sorry baby." I pushed him off me. "Get off me!" I yelled. "What the fuck Danity you know I love you." "Nigga your wife is my Mom's best friend! I keep telling you this cannot happen. My Mother came to me she knows, you know how embarrassing that shit is? Tre you need to leave me alone." He grabbed me and put his hand under my robe. His fingers found my wet pussy and he fondled me. "You want me to leave you alone?" It felt good, but I was not about to let a moan escaped. I pushed his hands away from me "yes." He stared at me in disbelief. "Bitch I own you, you belong to me." "Business wise but personally I belong to no one!" I threw up my ring finger. That pissed him off. There was a knock at the door. Tre went to answer it like he lived there. He opened the door and it was Tip. He looked pissed. I walked up to the door. "Hey baby my Uncle Tre was just leaving" I said as I pulled Tip into the door. Tre started laughing "alright Danity

I will see you later." He headed out the door. I rolled my eyes closed and locked the door. "Damn that nigga acting like y'all fucking." Tip said. I didn't even respond to him. Tip went straight to the bedroom he knew just what I needed. Tip came and fucked me just like I wanted. After the sex was over, I loved over at him. He knew it was time to go. Once, Tip left I called my Mother to make sure she was alright. She was hysterical crying and Crenshaw told me to let her rest and to call her tomorrow. I laid in the bed and stared at the ceiling. My phone vibrated and it was Uncle Tre. Uncle Tre 'I am sorry Danity but we need to be together' I didn't even answer I just ignored his text. Uncle Tre was getting overboard with what he was trying. There was no way that I could be with him. Sex was just sex there was nothing after that. The days rolled around the time to say good-bye to Auntie Mya came quickly. Auntie Mya's funeral was that Saturday. Tre had her looking very beautiful I must admit. Her long curly hair framed her small face. She looked older than what I was used too, and she was a shade dark. As the tears fell rapidly from my eyes, I kissed her on the cheek and told her I was sorry. The guilt I held in my heart would probably never go away. I walked away from the casket with a heavy heart. Maurice and Imani were there, and I must admit she complimented my brother well. My mother had Crenshaw and I had no one. I sat next to my brother. He held my hand. I hugged him and he hugged me back. I would always have my brother he loved me, and I loved him.

Chapter Twenty-Three
IMANI

I had fallen for Maurice. He was the sweetest man ever. I loved everything about him, and I wanted him to be with me forever. I even got close to this sister Danity. She was a loner and I didn't understand why because she was gentle and nice. She was going out of town for the weekend and she asked me to go with her. I accepted the invitation I didn't have any friends and I had nothing else to do. She honked the horn to her Challenger, and I headed out and locked the door. I kissed her cheek when I entered the car. "Hey sis" I said to her. She pulled off. She looked good in her red blazer. She had on a long black skirt. "Where we going to first?" She asked me. "The nail shop of course." I replied. Maurice had given me some money to go with Danity. He had even helped me with the daycare.

He hired more people so that I could have more time off. We went to get our feet and nails done. I wanted to do some girl talk with Danity. She was so quiet and reserved but I knew there was more to her. "So why don't you have a boyfriend?" I questioned Danity. "A boyfriend? Shit I do. Well Tip is not my boyfriend but we fucking." I almost choked on my gum. She said it so loud. The Asian ladies were looking at us now. "Damn girl okay I guess I shouldn't have assumed." I told her. "Damn right," she laughed. "So, are you pregnant?" "What why would you say that?" I asked her that question came out of nowhere. "Mama said she dreamed of some damn fishes and it for damn sure ain't me." She said. "I don't know to be honest. Hell, we have been you know doing it without protection." "Yeah your ass pregnant." She said. I started laughing. I had never thought I could be pregnant. Damn we hadn't been together that long. I wasn't sick or anything like that. I guess I would have to wait to see if my period came. We decided to grab lunch at Olive Garden. The waiter brought out our salads. We were chatting when their Uncle Tre walked in. I smiled at him and he walked right to our table. Danity didn't see him at first until he got closer. She rolled her eyes and smacked her lips. He came and sat next to me. "So, you are going through William now to get your assignments?" He started interrogating her. She didn't say anything to him. He hit the table with his fists, and it scared me "Answer me dammit!" The people in the restaurant were staring at us. I didn't know what to do. I grabbed my phone just in case I needed to call Maurice. "Yes, you act like you don't want to give me any work!" Danity yelled back at him. "Well your little trip for this weekend is cancelled. The only way you get work is through me!" He growled. "You can't do that!" She snapped back at him. "I can do what I want little girl." "Why are you acting like this?" She squinted her eyes with anger. "The same reason you are acting the way you are. Because I want too." "No, I am acting this way because I have morals!" He got up from the table "it's a little too late for that baby girl." He grabbed her under her chin and kissed her lips. I turned away I did not know what was going on. He left out of the restaurant. I didn't know what to say. "His sick ass," Danity picked up her phone. "Hello Will." Whoever she called had answered. "Yeah he came talking that shit!" She paused while he spoke, "okay." She hung up. "Girl sorry about that nasty ass Uncle Tre don't know how to let shit be. Talking about I ain't got to do the job tomorrow he a lie. I need my money." I didn't say anything as I ate the rest of my food. I did not know what was going on in this family. I was a bit uneasy after the altercation at the restaurant. I could tell Danity knew it, so she dropped me off once we got done eating. Once I got inside my house, I wondered did Maurice know his little sister was sleeping with their Uncle.

Chapter Twenty-Four
MAURICE

y daddy hit my mother over and over and she went to hide. I tried to help her, but he slapped me down. My mother came behind him and stabbed him in the back. I jumped out of my sleep in a horrible sweat. I looked down at Imani she was still sleeping. I rubbed her little baby bump. We had found out she was pregnant three months again. I was happy to become a father. I didn't know what was in store for me though. I had a fucked up past and I didn't even know where to start. My mother was always dating different men Crenshaw put an end to that. I remember a little bit about my father Hakeem. The most important and worst thing he used to beat on my Mother. I remembered it a little bit, but I was not that old, so the events are sketchy. I know the day that he died he slapped me down to the floor. I remember my mother taking up for me and telling me to hide in the bathroom. We had done it so many times before. There was a lock on the bathroom door so that is why my Mother always told us to go hide in there. That is all I remember is taking Danity in the bathroom with me and hiding. After that my father was dead. I needed answers and the only person who could give them to me was my mother. It seemed as if ever since Imani had told me she was pregnant I had these reoccurring nightmares of my father. I didn't know if it was a sign that I was going to be like him or what. The next morning, I made my way over to my Mother's house. My stepfather opened the door for me, "hey son," he greeted me. I gave him a weak smile. "Is Mom here?" "Yeah she in the kitchen making cookies." He told me as he locked the door. He headed to the back of the house and I headed towards the kitchen. As soon as my mother saw me, she got up and embraced me. "What brings my handsome son to see his Mama?" she said. "Oh, Mama stop acting like that." "Humph seem like since you got with Imani you been acting funny." She said. I knew she was going to say that. My mother and my sister were my life. I did everything with them and my stepdad. "It ain't even like that Ma." She started laughing "I know but I am a bit jealous." I didn't have time for the small talk. I blurted out my thoughts before our conversation become unnecessary chatter. "Ma what happened to Daddy? How did he die?" She turned around and looked at me. "He had an asthma attack." She said and quickly turned around. "Yeah but how did he have an asthma attack?" "I don't want to talk about your father." She said to me. "But Ma.." "No Malcolm I don't want to talk about it!" She threw down the pot and left out of the kitchen. I didn't think that bringing up my father would make her so mad. I picked the pot up from the floor and put it back in its place. I waited for the timer to go off on the cookies. I took them out. My stepfather appeared in the kitchen with me. "You upset your mother boy," he said as he grabbed a cookie. "I upset her? Shit I should be upset. All I asked her was what happened to my father?" "She had it hard with your father. I know you know that he used to beat her. Some things that we ask for is too much for us to handle. You know what you know and the rest you don't need to know. You understand boy?" I nodded my head in agreement. So basically, he was telling me that I didn't need to know so I should stop asking. They were making me get a headache. I got up and headed out to check on my weed. Business was booming as usual. The police had finally found Dee's body, but it was badly burned. Crenshaw had done a number on him to hide the evidence. Chastity called me with the news, and I pretended to give a fuck. They had the funeral and Iman and Danity attended with me. You should have seen the look on Chastity's face when she saw Imani. I didn't give a fuck I hadn't fucked with her in months. Imani was everything to me and more. I loved her and I was so happy that she was having my baby. I needed to go harder and make more money. My damn sister was making more money than me. I wanted to stay lowkey and off the grid, but that shit was costing me money. I needed to expand because my weed was grade A. Everyone in the city wanted to fuck with "the plug" as they called me. I just couldn't risk losing everything, and I also couldn't be scared to make shit happen. With a baby on the way I was starting a family and my dough had to be up. I knew a couple of niggas too that would help get this shit started. God, Redd, Bear, and Kj I knew them niggas would be down. I made a few calls to them niggas to set up a meeting. The Plug was about come out of hiding so niggas could know who ran this game. I knew Danity could line me up with some real bitches that would pop something, so it was time to make this money. I looked around at the pots of weeds that were growing it was time to make an entrance.

Chapter Twenty-Five
DANITY

When Maurice called and told me his plans, I was shocked the nigga was ready to do big thangs and he wanted to put me on his payroll. I was going to be done fucking with Uncle Tre and William. It wasn't going to be easy but there was always a price to get out of the game. I had been staying low ever since I got back from Oregon. The job I had to do was difficult I almost got caught. My assignment was for me to kill a cop. Not just any cop it was a cop that was heavily in the media. Stanley Pickerson had killed an innocent black man they said. This was going on a lot and black people were tired of hearing about it. His wife was the one who wanted him dead. Cynthia Pickerson was a black woman and she was at the end of her rope. Not only was her husband abusive but he told her that he shot that young boy on purpose. He wasn't being investigated or anything. When I take on a job, I never really care about the specifics it is my job to kill and that is all. I had seen him on the television that is how I knew who he was. So, when I had to stalk him that is when I gathered the other information. It was a pleasure sticking my machete through his body but as I sat in the back of the squad car another police car pulled up. What the hell did I expect? To my delight though he looked at the squad car and kept right on going that was a close call. Today I was going to get a little bit of maintenance done on my c ar. Crenshaw usually did it for me, but I was grown now I needed to do stuff on my own. I decided to check out this car shop on the Eastside. As I opened the door of the shop there h e st ood. 6'0, long dreads that had the tips a gold color, he had gold teeth and he was brown skinned. He was by far the fin est man I had ever seen and when I walked up close to him, I saw GOD tatted on his neck. He didn't see me behind him and bumped into me. "My bad beautiful" he said to me I blushed. I know my light skin was now red. "It's okay." He was about to walk away when he turned back around. "I'm God," his sexy voice hit me, and I damn near had an orgasm. "I am Danity nice to meet you." I gave him my hand and he kissed it. I was really blushing now. "Shit can I take you out sometime?" Hell yeah, I thought but I had to play it cool "sure." I told him. He handed me his Iphone, and I put my number in it. He grabbed the phone and called my number. "Now you got my number alright." He said to me. He walked out of the shop and I was still mesmerized. The lady at the counter had to bring me back to reality as I watched my future man ride away. "He fine ain't he." She said. I looked at the girl and got back to business "I need a tune up and oil change." I said to her. I was not about have a conversation with this woman, but I would be calling my brother to see if he knew this God character. UUUUUUGGGGGGHHHHH!! Maurice had pissed me off. So of course, I call him and ask him if he knew God. Of course, his high yella ass know everybody and do you know he had the nerve to say to me. He told me not t o be a hoe and that he wanted God on his team. HUUUU UUHHHH! He acted like I was just some damn hoe. I had n ever fucked a ny of his friends. Damn I fucked Uncle Tre and now I am labeled as a hoe? What made it so bad God h ad been texting me for a week straight and I did not answer. I didn't want to disappoint my brother. God 'damn you don't like me beautiful?' I wanted to reply so damn bad and let him know. Shit I think I love you and I barely know you. Maurice was so damn evil. HUUUUUUH!!! I loved my broth er and I tried to be respe ctful. I went to the phone company and changed my number, but I kept God's name in my phone just in case Maurice changed his mind. William and Uncle Tre had been calling me also, so that was another great reason to change my number. I was no longer working for either one of them. I would deal with the consequences when they came to me. Maurice called the first meeting and I was running late. Tip had come, to scratch my itch earlier. He had fucked me so good I accidently fell back to sleep. I quickly had gotten dressed and got into my car. Maurice want ed the meeting at some damn office he was renting out downtown. I lived not too far but I was going to be noticeably late. I made it to the elevator and hit the fifth floor that is where Maurice told me to meet him. There were all different offices but there was only one that did not have a name on it. I was guessing it was Maurice's. I knocked on the door. "Come in Danity!" He said with more authority than I was used too. "Sorr..."I couldn't even finish my sentence. Crenshaw, and three other guys were sitting at the table that I did not recognize but I recognized him, God. I didn't even finish my word as I made my way in the room. I could tell that everyone was loving the sight of me. I sat in the seat on the left side of Maurice. "Sit to my right." He ordered me. I don't know why he was being so bossy, but I got up and did as I was told. "I wanted Danity to sit on the right side of me because she is my right hand. Yup this little petite beautiful woman is my right hand. Anybody got a problem?" No, one said anything. I was honored to be considered my brother's right-hand man, well woman "Okay let's start off with introductions. Danity of course is first this is my lovely sister and she is deadly she will be security. Do you have any women yet?" "Yes, I do I didn't know they were supposed to come." "No worries sis they weren't I just wanted to make sure you up on your job. This my Pops Crenshaw and he is leading me he knows the game very well. Any shit you can't get in to contact with me about come to him. If he not available, then you go to Danity. Now you, niggas can introduce yourselves." The guy with the blue suit stood up and I rolled my eyes how the fuck did Maurice find him? "I am Kj. I am security on the streets from what Maurice explained to me. Danity will be the security underground I will be the one out here on the streets my crew will get shit handled everytime." He sat down he was a cute brown skinned guy, but he had a big ass head. "I am Redd I will be organizing shit with the workers. Niggas will make this money and bring shit back the right way," he said damn he was a cutie too. He was light skinned with some starter dreads in his head. "Niggas already know I ain't fucking around. I am going to be helping my nigga with the growth of the product. This shit is very scientific trust I smoked some of this nigga's weed and it is potent and will get you high. This shit is going to set the city on the map." The little dark-skinned guy said. "Tell your name nigga." Maurice said. "Bear." We all had to laugh at him shit he was not even that big and somebody named him Bear. "Aye niggas I was a fat baby." That made us laugh even harder. God was up next, and I smiled. I wondered who he was and what he was about. "God. I was going to be the competition until Maurice brought me on. I been running shit on the Eastside for a minute. I am ready to expand." He said and sat down. He hadn't even said shit and I was dazed. Damn why was he so fine? "Danity talk to em baby." Maurice commanded. I didn't know what to say shit Maurice had not told me shit I stood anyway. My white blazer was hugging me tight and I had on some black jeans. "I am Danity and I guess I will be taking care of the heavyweight." Bear laughed. I cut my eyes at him. Was he laughing because I was so beautiful and young? Maurice noticed that he was laughing at me and grabbed my hand for me to sit down. "Bear don't laugh or underestimate the power of her she is a killer nigga." I did a simple motion with my hand to snatch the dart from behind my ear. I slung it quick, hard, and fast as it, stung Bear right in his left arm. He screamed out in pain. I drew my pistol and dared him to move. "The next time you laugh nigga be prepared for the consequences." I said as I steadied my pistol at him. He looked on in horror. "That's all you need bro?" I asked Maurice. "Yeah you can go Danity." He knew I was pissed and in kill mode. I put my pistol back in my purse and walked out of the room. Bear had pissed me off. As I closed the door, I heard Kj. "Dammmmnnn! Your sister fine Maurice." "Don't be looking at my sister nigga." He said to him.

Chapter Twenty-Six
MAURICE

⟶ ∘»»❂«❂«∘ ⟵

My first meeting was a success except for Danity having to check that nigga Bear. Other than that shit was good. Danity told me to meet her at the office because she was bringing the girls by. Imani wanted to go with me, but I told her she had to stay at home. I had told her a little of my plans and she was not for it, but what could she do I was the man. I dressed in my khaki slacks with my aqua green button up. I pulled into the parking space when I got a call from God. "What up?" "Shit nigga where you at?" "Pulling up to the office right now." "Cool I will be there in a second I got some shit I want to tell you." "Cool" we hung up. I made my way to the fifth floor. I was at the office door and I heard music playing in there like they were having a party. I opened the door without knocking. All I saw was ass. This girl had the fattest ass I had ever seen. She was a BBW for sure and I can tell you that ass was moving. "Get your ass down off my table." I yelled at her. Danity cut the music. "Damn bro why you didn't knock?" "Knock in my office stop it." I grabbed the girl's hand and helped her down. She was fine as hell. She had a red bob in, and it complimented her caramel skin well. She sat down in the seat and I went to the head of the table. "Ladies this is not a game don't be in my damn office acting a fool." "It was my fault bro." Danity owned up to it. "Anyways this is Cherry Bomb and Lexxi." Cherry Bomb was the fine ass BBW and Lexxi was an Asian beauty. She had long hair and she was thick too, but she wasn't as stacked as Cherry Bomb. "Hey ladies I am Maurice your bosses's boss." I laughed to break the ice. "Do y'all know why y'all are here?" "Yes, to take out the heavyweight." Lexxi said she surprised me because she didn't sound Asian at all. There was a knock at the door I told God to come in. He came in and looked at the ladies. I know he was trying to see if he should talk about business. "These are the heavy hitters right here God they are working under Danity. Meet Cherry Bomb and Lexxi." "Oh, straight so these ladies are the ones I need to be talking to anyway." I looked at him quizzically "what you mean?" "My young solider came to me last night and told me that some niggas have been asking him who is his plug? Now I know we just getting started but apparently there is some type of political nigga who supposed to get a percentage of our money. This shit is all new to me." Shit it was new to me too. "Well his name is William." Danity spoke I knew that was her boss but what the fuck did that have to do with us? "William thinks that all crime can be erased if you pay him. He is the police chief. I work for him from time to time. That is who Tre is connected with." She looked at me. "Damn the police chief a damn dirty cop no wonder so much crime be going on." God said. "So, he thinks that I am supposed to give him a percentage of my business? Fuck that Danity you need to take care of that problem sis." "What you mean?" She sounded scared. "Just what I said. Sis he is going to be a problem I need you to take care of him. You know that nigga personally get it done." She nodded her head. "You gone need some help?" God asked her. "Maybe." She said. I didn't like the look they were giving each other. "Hit me up my number ain't changed." Oh shit. I had to interrupt "okay shit is that all my nigga?" "Yeah I just wanted you to know shit before it happened." "Good looking out." I gave him dap and he headed out. I saw the nigga make a damn call me sign to Danity she sat there smiling. As soon as he closed the door, I let her ass know. "Yup and only call him for business no extra shit." She rolled her eyes and turned back on the music that was my cue to go. Cherry Bomb looked at me to make sure it was okay to get up and dance. "Y'all ladies have fun." I told them as I headed out. I made sure to glance back at Cherry Bomb damn she had a fat ass. Danity caught me looking and rubbed her belly. I flipped her the bird. I knew I had Imani at home and she was pregnant, but I still wanted to glance at Cherry's big ass.

DANITY

I was tired of Maurice cock blocking ass. I saw him looking at Cherry that day all up in that big ole ass. I knew that Cherry and Lexxi would be the perfect girls for the job. Cherry was one of Uncle Tre's side pieces that used to work with us. She bought herself out of her contract. She said it was easy she said she had so much dirt on Williams that he was going to be an easy target. Lexxi was a girl that she knew. They did jobs together before. Lexxi was a free agent so she was down for whatever. I had contemplated calling God, but I was not sure what to say. We really didn't need his help, but I wanted an excuse to call him. I threw caution to the wind and dialed his number. It rang five times and I was going to hang up when he picked up. "Hello" I said into the phone. "Hello," it was a woman I looked down at the number I had dialed the right number. "Ummm can I speak with God?" "See you still got bitches calling you nigga. That's what the fuck I am talking about." There was a noise and then he got on the phone. "Who this?" He calmly asked. "It's me Danity." "Aw what up you ready to talk business?" "Yeah" I said feeling a bit heartbroken. "Alright where you live at?" I shot him my address and went to put on some ugly clothes. I was not looking cute for someone else's man. I didn't even know what I was going to say now. I was too damn salty he already had a woman. I was trying to gather my thoughts when there was a knock on my door. It was God of course and he was looking good as hell. I closed and locked the door behind him. "What up lil mama you got a plan huh?" He smelled great as his cologne filled my nostrils. "Yeah" I mumbled. I sat on the love seat and he sat next to me like there wasn't a whole empty couch. "So, Cherry knows that William likes to cheat on his wife on Thursdays. He has a bitch that he goes to fuck on. We know where she stays and everything. We are just going to get his ass over there. She got a nigga and everything so we could make it seem like he got them." "Sounds smooth but what you want my soldiers to do?" I didn't say anything because I didn't have answer. He smiled at me I had been busted. "You just wanted to see me, didn't you?" I rolled my eyes "don't flatter yourself nigga." He put his hand on my thigh and I kindly removed it. "I just wanted to know if my idea was good?" "Yeah lil mama that shit straight you know what you are doing." He got up. "Where are you going?" I asked fast and I knew I sounded desperate. "I am about to head out shit my bitch already tripping on me." I rolled my eyes so damn hard they almost got stuck "well bye." He started laughing. I opened the door for him. He walked out the door and turned to me "Is your mad or nah?" I slammed the door in his face. I heard him laughing. Hell yeah, I was big mad hell. Ugggghhhh damn Maurice, but I had dodged a bullet because he already had a woman. I ran to the phone and dialed Tip. Shit he would satisfy me every time I saw God, I had to make the call to him. Two hours later I rolled off Tip. He was staring at me as I laid on the bed next to him. "You must be checking for some nigga?" "Excuse me?" I did not know what the fuck he was talking about. "I don't know Dan it's like you be fucking the shit of me lately. Is it because you can't fuck the nigga you really want to fuck?" "Bye Tip." I said to him he had pissed me off. His phone rung before he could respond to me. I got up and got dressed. I wasn't really paying attention to his conversation until I heard him say God. I knew Tip hustled, but I never really got into his business he was just a friendly fuck. He hung up the phone and I had not caught a word of the conversation. "Who was that?" I questioned him. He started laughing "God my boss but you knew that already." I turned to him. What the fuck was he trying to say? "Yeah I saw your number in that nigga phone. I know it was recently that you gave him your numb er because you just got this number. He must be nigga you be fantasizing about. You be saying Oh my God too many times for me." This nigga had lost his mind. "Tip it ain't even like that." "Yeah whatever bitch he got a bitch anyway. Why you want him and she way badder than you." I could not believe he said that shit "get the fuck out Tip!" I screamed. He got up and headed out the door I followed him I was about to lock my door. He opened the door and when I got near, he, backhanded me I held my face in shock. "Dumb bitch." He walked out of the apartment. I closed the door. I could not believe that Tip would slap me like that. I was mad at him, but I was angry at God. He had a bitch and she was badder than me? I went back into my room and dialed his number. "What up?" "You that's what up. So, you think your bitch look better than me huh?" I said into the phone. "Danity what the fuck is you talking about?" "Yeah Tip told me you got a bitch and she finer than me. Then he called me a dumb bitch and slapped me." "He did what?" He growled into the phone. "Nah nigga you did what. So, your bitch is better than me?" I questioned. "Danity you need to calm down. You know I was feeling you. You the one who didn't call me back remember." "Yeah because my brother knew you, but I was feeling you too." I confessed. Just then I heard another voice "You damn right I told your ass to stop being a hoe. You fucking Tip too damn Danity." It was Maurice. Damn! I hung up the phone. God had me on damn speaker phone. HUH! Now I was going to have to hear Maurice's mouth again. My phone started ringing I saw that it was God and I pressed ignore. He tried to call three more times and I ignored them. He sent a text. God 'that nigga hit you?' I smiled he was worried about me. Me 'yes' I waited for a notification from a text, but he didn't text back. I don't know why God had me on speaker, but I was pissed. Other than that, I got the vibe that he really cared about me. I was happy that I had called him, but I was not trying to deal with Maurice.

It had been months since I buried my wife Mya. The shit was hard but what was even harder was the way that Danity was treating me. She had not given me any pussy in so damn long and I was having withdrawals. Just thinking about staring into those gray eyes made my dick hard. Besides I need her comfort at a time like this. William had been killed. My boss William had been on the scene for over 20 years. William was the damn chief of police who would dare kill him? Julian had called himself trying to figure out who "the plug" was, but shit that mission was at a standstill. We needed to find out who the hell had killed William. Jack was William's boss and he was pissed, I knew he was pissed when he personally called me. I didn't know what to say and I did not know how business was going to go. The next chief of police was not on our roster of crooked cops. Many of our dealings were going to have be stopped because we couldn't get caught. I picked up my phone and dialed Danity's number for the tenth time. She was a distraction I needed her bad. For the tenth time she sent me to the voicemail, once she knew I had gotten her new number she started ignoring my calls. Damn she was getting on my nerves. What she didn't know was that I was sitting outside of her apartment. I wasn't stalking her just keeping an eye on what she was doing. I saw some nigga with golds come in her apartment. Then like an hour later that other nigga she had been fucking with came. Danity was a hoe but I wanted her she was gorgeous. I looked at my phone and pulled up her picture. Everything about her was beautiful damn. I knew I could change her ways if only she would allow me. My phone rang and I was pissed it interrupted my thoughts. "Hello," I bellowed into the phone. "They appointed Bart Martin to be chief of police." Jack said into the phone. "So?" I questioned. We already knew that was coming. "He is not about to be with this shit. He is a problem, get rid of him!" He shouted. "Aight," I hung up the phone I didn't need any more words. Ten minutes later Jack emailed me Bart's information. I was itching to get some stress off. As I drove to my destination, I got an incoming call I looked down and I was surprised to see that it was Danity. I answered right away. "Hello." I quickly answered I didn't want her to hang up. "Yeah you keep calling me?" I could hear she was annoyed. "Yeah I got some work for you." I tried to make it all about money. She smacked her lips "I no longer work for you remember and since William is dead I..." She was pissing me off. I cut her off "bitch you belong to me!" I growled. "No, the fuck I don't!" she yelled into the phone "BITCH!!" "Fuck you Danity." I hung up in her face. She was crazy out her mind. She knew how this shit went. I pulled up to the house where Bart lived. It was a nice quiet block. It was hot and I needed to get this job done fast. The tinted windows were excellent for the job that I was doing. I had stolen this car earlier so that I could watch Danity's house without her knowing it was me. This had worked out perfectly. I thought I was going to have to do a fake break-in, but just as I was getting out the care Bart came walking out the house. He was smiling as he swung a baby's car seat. He was a proud father, I could tell. I aimed my gun at the closed window. I lowered the window and he didn't know what hit him. BANG! The bullet ripped through his forehead. I had the perfect aim. His body and the car seat hit the ground and I could hear the baby crying. I was about to pull off when a woman hysterically came running out of the house. I let off a round and hit her in the chest as she ran towards her husband. I put the car in drive and speed away, I know neighbors had heard the shots and would be calling the police. Later that day I was in my house eating some fruit when there was breaking news. I knew it was going to be about Bart. Sure, as hell they were talking about the shooting. I was smiling as I bit into the watermelon that is until they said that his wife had survived. Like clockwork my phone started ringing and it was Jack. "Hello," I hesitantly answered. "You missed." Was his greeting. "I see. I will finish it." I reassured him. "I already got my man on it. Lay low I don't know if they know who you are. Did she see your face?" "I had on a mask," I breathed in deep. "Lay low." Was all he said before he hung up. I fell back against the couch, damn I had never missed my target, ever. I didn't know if a neighbor or anyone had seen my face before I put on the mask. I dialed Danity's number and once again she did not answer. This shit was driving me crazy. I had to get out of here. Laying low for me I knew that I had to really disappear. I wanted Danity to leave with me, but she wasn't answering. I quickly made my way to the bedroom and opened my suitcase. I packed my clothes as much as I could, grabbed my safe, and the picture of Mya and I. I went to the garage and grabbed the gasoline that I used to fill up the lawnmower. I went back inside and poured gasoline in each room. I called a taxi as I saturated the house. Once the taxi driver called to tell me they were in the front I did what I had to do. I lit the match in the back bedroom and opened all the doors. I locked the front door as if nothing was going on. I had to make a clean getaway. I was going back to Milwaukee I had a house there and I knew my way around the city. I had moved to Cali with Mya and her friend anyways. Now she was gone, and I could get back to assignments in the Midwest. Once the taxi driver dropped me off at the airport I paid for my ticket. I got situated as I waited for my flight. I dialed Jack's number to let him know I was doing what I was told. He answered on the first ring. I made the call "I am getting ghost." I said into the phone. "Good keep in touch." Jack said to me.

Chapter Twenty-Eight

MAURICE

I slammed the knife into this hand. I could hear his bone crack and his flesh rip apart. "ARRRGGGH!" He screamed out in pain. "Shut the fuck up!" God screamed. His voiced boomed and I jumped. We had fucked Tip up. I didn't know what the fuck was going on with Danity. She knew better than to let some nigga, but his hands on her. Since she didn't want to handle him, we would. That is what God told me when he brought Tip to the warehouse. We had beat his ass and tortured him a bit, but he was alive. God punched Tip over and over in his face. He was in a chair with his arms tied down. Tip was yelping out in pain and the blood was spewing from this mouth, nose, and lips. "You like hitting women nigga? You like telling my business too I see." He was hitting the nigga so hard I could hear his jaw break. I pulled him off the nigga. "Calm down nigga." "I got this shit! Nigga you all calm this is a disrespectful ass nigga!" I didn't know if God was mad because Tip had told Danity about his bitch. Or if he was mad about him hitting her. I was guessing it was because of the information he had told her. I on the other handed wanted him to learn never to hit my sister. "So, you want this nigga dead?" God questioned. The veins in his neck were pulsating and I could tell he was thirsty for blood. I shook my head. "Nah shit I just want to beat his ass." I never wanted him to die. God walked up to me. "Nigga he gots to go! Shit he not gone let us forget this shit!" God knew Tip better than I did. He had worked with him long enough he knew what he was capable of. He took his pistol out of his waistband. "Kill that nigga," he demanded. I didn't say anything to him as he handed me the pistol. I had never killed anyone. I think he could sense I was scared. I remember Danity told me never to kill because it would change me. I had seen her kill and I knew she had plenty of blood on her hands. If she could do it then why couldn't I? I was a man I was built for this shit. Plus, he had put his hands on my little sister he deserved to die. I aimed the gun at Tip. He stared at me and spit blood onto the floor. God had done a number on him. His face was badly bruised, and he didn't look like the guy that was brought into the warehouse. I didn't know if it was fear or anger that was in his eyes. Tip lunged his body at me. My body tensed and I squeezed the trigger with my eyes closed. "Arrrgh!" He cried out as I opened my eyes. My heart was beating fast as I looked at Tip gasping for air. God hit my shoulder, "finish that nigga off." God told me. My eyes were wide with panic. I was scared I did not know what I had just done, but I wanted to put him out of his misery. I looked back at Tip as his chest heaved up and down, I brought the gun up again and pulled the trigger. I missed the first time and hit the chair. I repositioned the pistol so that I could make it quick. I aimed for the forehead and fired. His brains splatted all over the floor and his head fell down. His skull was exposed, and blood, bones, and brains were everywhere. I was shaking and I could feel my breakfast coming up. I couldn't contain it as I emptied my guts over the floor. God jumped back. "Ugh! What the fuck nigga! This your first kill?" God asked. I didn't say anything as I continued to empty my stomach of its contents. Once I got control of myself, I made my way out of the warehouse. I was wobbling as I climbed into my car. I quickly started up my car as sweat dripped down my face. I nearly had three accidents, but I made it home safely. She was sitting in the living room with her feet up. She could see the look on my face. "What's wrong baby?"

She jumped up and came to me. "I need some water" I said shaking. She ran to the kitchen to get me some water. I staggered to the bedroom and I stripped out of my clothes. My body was sweaty as I lay across the bed. Imani came back into the bedroom with the water. I had my eyes closed as I tried to think of something other than Tip's head exploding because of me. "Baby you alright?" She asked me. I opened my eyes and was about to reach for the water. I looked at Imani and her head exploded. "Aggggggghhhhh!" I screamed as pushed her away from me. The water splashed over my hot body I closed my eyes. "What the fuck is wrong with you?" She questioned. I opened my eyes again and it was Imani, and nothing was wrong with her head. "Get the fuck out!" I hollered at her. I needed to be alone. "What?" She asked me. "Just go in the living room Imani!" I demanded. She was confused, but she did as she was told. She closed the bedroom door and I cuddled with my blanket. My stomach was in knots. Who knew killing a nigga would do this to me? I had seen dead bodies and people getting killed in front of me. It was something about being on the other side of that gun. Danity had warned me I closed my eyes and once again Tip's head exploded, and brains splattered everywhere. I jumped out of the bed with my eyes open. I was breathing heavy and my body was drenched with sweat. I was panting and grunting as I paced the floor. I slapped my temples because I had to get that vision out my head. I looked in the mirror on my dresser. I looked like a totally different person. I stared to long and in the reflection of the mirror I saw Tip's head exploding again. I jumped back into the bed. "No!" I cried out. Imani swung the door open, "bae is you okay?" I had my eyes closed tightly. "Call Danity! Call my sister!"

Chapter Twenty-Nine
DANITY

When Imani called me, I thought she was calling to kick it. When she told that something was wrong with Maurice I immediately panicked and hauled ass to his house. I didn't know what was going on. As soon as I made it to the house Imani was sitting on the couch crying. My heart fell into my stomach was he dead? "Where Reese?" I dreaded to ask. "In the room," she cried I felt bad for her and wanted to console her, but my brother came first. I walked into the room and he was sleep. I climbed in the bed with him and held him. His pillow was soaked so he had to been crying. His body was a sweaty mess. I guess my movement woke him up. He smiled when he saw me his eyes were blood shot red. "What's wrong bro?" I questioned. He closed his eyes and the tears fell "I killed him," he said. I now understood I hugged him and let the tears fall. I knew how it was to have blood on your hands. The feeling was not good . It did something for me it satisfied me, but Maurice was not like me he was kindhearted. He was a thug, but he was no killer. "It's going to be alright? Who was it?" I gently rocked him. "Tip me and God..." I shushed him. "It's okay it will be okay. Just remember that he is not you and that you had to do what you had to do." I rocked my big brother in my arms, and he fell back to sleep. I sat in the bed awhile and watched him sleep. I had told him not to do it. I had a craving to kill yet it still haunted me when I took a life. He would eventually get through it, but he would never be the same. I told Imani to call me if Reese needed anything. Once I got in my car, I called Crenshaw. "Hello Pops." "Danity, what's wrong?" He asked I guess he could hear the worry in my voice. "Maurice, he has blood on his hands." I told him as tears ran down my face. "What?" "He at the house now sleep. I just left him, he fucked up." I said as I wiped my tears. "Alright." Was all the Crenshaw said. I hung up the phone and looked down at my phone. This situation was giving me mixed emotions. I was sad and mad at the same time. One emotion that I could always turn to was anger. I started up my car and sped to my destination. When I made it in front of Auntie Mya's house I was in disbelief. The house was burned to the ground. When did this happen? I knew what this meant Tre was trying to disappear. That was fine with me because as soon as I saw his ass, I was going to kill him. Someone had to feel my anger and since Tre had gotten ghost, I was going to turn to someone else, God. I knew where he stayed. I made my way to his house. I saw his gold car and knew that he was home. I walked through the grass. It was eerily quiet, and the clacking of my heels was scaring me. I saw that his living room light was on. I knocked on the door. The gorgeous woman who answered the door took me by surprise. She was my color with a big face. Her hair was tied in a scarf and she did not look happy to see me. I didn't say any words I just punched her in her face. She stumbled back. I punched her again and kicked her in the stomach. I know my heels hurt her stomach she doubled over in pain. She fell to the ground and God came running towards me, I drew my pistol he stopped. "What the fuck Danity!" He growled. "Tell her she has to go!" I yelled. "What?" He asked. He was sexy. His shirt was off, and I could see all the tattoos that covered his body. It made me think of August Alsina's song "kissing on my tattoos". I shook the thought out of my head. "Tell her to go!" I demanded again. "Ebony gone head and go." He helped her off the floor. She looked at me and I could tell she was scared. She had got up and grabbed her purse. She left out the house with no hoes on. We heard her car start up and she drove away. I still had my gun drawn. "You son of a bitch why did you let him kill him?" I glared into his eyes. At firs t, he had no emotions but that quickly changed into a smile . "What do you mean?" "You know damn well what I mean! He is not like me and you! He is not a killer he is a hustler, but he is not a killer!" God started walking towards me "stop where you at!" I told him. "I ain't on shit" he said as he got close to me. I put the gun down "why would you let him experience that?" The tears slipped from my eyes. The hurt I felt for my brother was indescribable. It was like the first time I had killed for Uncle Tre. I closed my eyes as I shook away the image. God grabbed my waist and pulled me to him. I opened my eyes. "He wanted to play with the big boys then he needs to get r eady." He kissed me. DAMMMMNNN! His lips felt soft like Vaseline coating my lips on a cold ass winter day. "But he was not ready." He kissed me again and my knees gave out, but he caught me. "No one ever is," he spoke the truth. He kissed me long and passionate.

Damn he was making me wet. I rubbed my hands all over his body. That song came to my mind again. He let me go. "Why you come over here acting up and shit." He smacked my butt. I didn't say anything to him I just admired his beauty. "You hear me talking to you girl?" I smacked my lips at him "girl? I am a grown ass woman." He shook his head "nah a grown ass woman would have come over here and told me to fuck her cause that's what you really want." That statement sent me through the roof. My panties were soaked and were seeping through my damn pants. I just stood there taking in his sexiness. He was staring me down and I could see the lust in his eyes. He reached for my hand. I didn't give it to him. He snatched me up and kissed my neck. He released me and guided me to his room. We walked in his bedroom and I dropped to my knees. He pulled his pants down and your girl was not disappointed. I took him into my mouth, and he tasted salty sweet. I grabbed his balls and made sure to rub them to warm them up. "Damn you sure know what you are doing." God moaned. I relaxed my throat to ease him in me more. He let out a scream and I felt that he was coming. I moved my mouth as his nut fell on my damn shirt. I could not believe he came that damn quick. I got up and was about to leave when he grabbed me and threw me on the bed. "Oh, you think you gone suck me and make me cum that quick." He pulled my pants off. "You done embarrassed the fuck out of me." I started laughing until he put his tongue on my damn clitoris. "Ummm." He held onto it and sucked on my pearl tongue. He knew what he was doing as he inserted his finger into my opening. "DAAAMMMMNNN!" I screamed. I tried to run because I was feeling like I had to pee. He held on to my clitoris and nippled on it, I couldn't take it any longer as I released. I squirted over his face and my body shook with pleasure. "I am sorry" I moaned. He got up with my cum on his face. "You sorry for what?" Now I felt embarrassed. "That was your first-time squirting wasn't it?" I didn't answer him, but he didn't seem to mind. He grabbed me by the ankles and spread my legs. He entered me fast and deeply. "OOOOOHHHHH!" I screamed. "Damn this pussy wet. I can see why Tip had to slap your ass." He thrust in and out of me and his motions were intoxicating. He thought he was going to get the best of me. I had to get control of myself. I felt my pussy muscles contracting. "OOOOOHHHHH baby this shit is so good." He kissed me "I know it is you my bitch?" "You already got a bitch" I moaned. He stopped. "Turn over" he instructed me. I got on all fours and put my ass in the air. He kissed my left cheek and then my right cheek. Damn my pussy was dripping. He entered me from behind. "Oh my GOD!" I cried out. "Yeah that's right throw that shit back." He pulled my long hair. I tried to throw it back but when I did, I had an orgasm "oooohhhh!" I moaned. "Get control of yourself girl. You my bitch?" He questioned me again. "I already told you." I said through my moans. "Oh, so you want to act stupid and shit?" He grabbed my waist and started ramming in me. "OH!OH!OH!OH! YESSSS! I AM! I AM!" I screamed. "You are what?" He teased me. He stopped and played with my nipples. "I am your bitch" I said between breaths. "That's right" he slowly stroked me. He had calmed down and I started throwing it back on him. I wanted to take control. He could tell. We changed positions and I got on top. I sat on his dick and bounced up and down. He held onto my hips and pounded in me. I kept bouncing and matching his rhythm. His eyes bucked out of his head and I knew he was about to cum. I swirled my hips and he was done for. I laid on his chest as we tried to catch our breath. I looked up at him. "Next time you want some dick just ask. You ain't got to come pulling out your pistol and shit." He laughed. I had to laugh too. I was satisfied but I still worried about my brother. I think

God could tell. "He gone be alright lil mama. He gone get through this situation and he gone be alright with me and you." I didn't say anything as I closed my eyes. I hoped he was right. My mind played back to when I was fourteen years old and the man tried to kill Uncle Tre. I felt my finger pull the trigger and I watched as his body dropped. I squeezed tightly onto God as I laid in his arms, these nightmares would never go away.

Chapter Thirty

AMBER

My baby had taken a life and he was hurt. When we walked into the room he was looking fucked up. I could not believe that he had experienced this. Was it something implanted in my DNA? Danity killed for a living and now my son had experienced it. Imani was in the living room looking scared. He needed to pull his self together for the girl. She was damn near due and he was losing his mind. I walked up to him and hugged him, and he hugged me back. His eyes were blood shot red and I knew that he was having a hard time. Crenshaw hugged him and told me to leave out the room. I didn't know what they were talking about, but I took this time to speak with Imani. She was a pretty girl with long dread locks. Pregnancy looked well on her. "Imani why you never talk about your parents?" She had never spoke about her family. I had only met her a couple of times, but she had never said anything about her family those couple of times. She laughed "I don't have any." She stated. "We all have parents." "Yeah well where are yours?" She questioned with an attitude. "Well my mother killed herself and I never knew my father." "So, you don't have any parents either?" She smacked her lips. "Yes, I do. One is deceased and one is missing. They don't mean that they are nonexistent." She looked at me and I saw the tears starting "my father raped me, and my mother allowed it." I grabbed her and hugged her. "I understand." She pushed me off her "you don't understand you don't know what I have been through." "Excuse the hell out of me, but you don't know what I have been through little girl. I am twice your age and I have been through hell and back. Don't you dare tell me what I don't know. I asked you because you are becoming a part of our family, but you will not disrespect me." She sat there looking sad "I am sorry." "Yeah I bet." I said as I went to the kitchen and grabbed a cup of juice. Imani followed me. "No, I am really sorry. I didn't mean anything by it. It is just that ever since Maurice has come home, he has been in the room, and won't let me in. But he will let you guys in and

Danity." "We are his family." I said in between swallows. "Oh, so I am not his family?" She questioned. "Yes, you are but you don't know what us as a family has went through. He is going through something right now, but he loves you." She smiled at that. She walked up to me and hugged me. I shook my head this girl had pregnancy emotions. We heard a knock on the door, and it was Danity. She looked rather refreshed and she had the finest piece of man with her. "Hey Ma." She hugged me. "Hey baby who is this?" I got right to the point. "This is God." She said. I looked at the girl like she was crazy. Did she just call this boy God? He was not my GOD. "Ma'am my name is Garrett Johnson." He reached out and shook my hand. I saw Danity roll her eyes at him. I knew that girl didn't even know his name, but I bet she had let him fuck her two ways to Sunday. "Okay hello. Crenshaw is in the room with Maurice." "Oh, okay good. I was coming to check on him, but I see he in good hands." "Girl please you know he is still going to want to see you." Crenshaw walked out of the room and it looked like he had the weight of the world on his head. "This is my husband Crenshaw." I introduced him to Garrett. They shook hands. "He wants to see you Amber." Crenshaw said to me. I let out a breath. I departed from the three and I walked into the room and he looked better. I think he even washed his face. "Mama I have failed you." He cried. "No why you say that?" I hurried to him. He was sitting in the bed and I sat next to him. I grabbed his hand. "You don't want me to be selling drugs and killing people. That ain't what you had in store for your kids." "So, you finally admitting you are a drug dealer?" I laughed to lighten the mood. He didn't smile though I breathed in deep. "Look son I know that our life was not ideal when you were younger and that your Auntie Mya was your stability. There are some things that I am not ready to face right now. I have buried away things, but just know that I will love you regardless. You are my son and you will never fail me." He gave ma kiss on the cheek "thanks mommy." "You are welcome son and if you ever need anything you let me know." I wanted to let him know I was in his corner one hundred percent. My son and daughter could be anything in this world. I had millions of dollars and I could build them businesses from the ground, but they wanted this life. I had killed their father, my ex-boyfriend, and my ex-husband so I couldn't judge. I was kind of like a black widow. I kissed my son good-bye. He came out of the room with me and hugged his sister and shook Garrett's hand. Crenshaw and I got in our Range Rover. I put the shades on my face to hide the tears. My life had not been perfect, but I never expected my kids to turn out this way. I had raised them, but the streets paid them more than love could ever amount too. It wasn't what I wanted, but I had to accept it because I had done so much dirt. The sins of a mother may fall onto their children. I never pictured our life would be this way.

3 MONTHS LATER...

Chapter Thirty-One

AMBER

This bitch had me meeting her in this dark ass office I was too old for this shit. I hadn't heard from her since she had come to California and asked me for some money. Now here she was again with the same bullshit. I didn't have time for it. I walked into the office and sat down at the desk. "What do you want Quita?" She did not put any fear into my heart. She smiled. She still looked good for her ass to be damn near fifty. I could tell she had died her edges so I could not see the gray, but I knew her age and I knew her. "Nice to see you too." She smiled. I quickly stood up because my blood was boiling. "I don't have time for this shit!" I yelled and turned to walk away. As I opened the door Tre walked into my path. I was not expecting to see him. The house that he and Mya had lived in had burned down months ago. No one had heard from him. "Hey long time no see." He said. "What is all this bullshit y'all?" I questioned. As soon as the words left my mouth a familiar face appeared behind Tre. It was Cedes. My blood was boiling over with anger. "Now why you want to be so mean? Tell us what is going on with your children?" Tre questioned. He was in my face and I could smell the pussy on his breath. "Y'all want to meet me to ask me what the fuck is going on with my damn kids?" I rolled my eyes. I knew what was going on with my children, but I wasn't going to tell them. After Maurice had caught his first body, he had gotten himself together. He was now running shit on the streets and Danity was helping him. They were making money and although it was not what I wanted I was proud of them. "Bitch you better tell me everything!" He demanded as he wrapped his hands around my neck. I struggled to breath as he squeezed tightly. Suddenly a shot rang out BANG! Was all I heard as Tre's grip loosened from around my neck. His body hit the floor. Mercedes started running and another shot rang out. Her body fell to the ground. I quickly got myself together and grabbed my gun from around my waist. Quita was screaming as Danity held the gun to her face. I ran to where Mercedes was on the ground crawling. I grabbed her ankles and pulled her back to the office. She was screaming and clawing at the floor, but I was stronger than her. I flipped her around and slapped her face. "Bitch what the fuck did you think you were doing?" I asked. Her eyes were scared. "It was Tre and Quita. They got me out of jail and told me that they had a plan to bring you down. I never wanted this." "Bitch fuck you," I said as I shot her in her chest. I turned my attention to Quita. I slowly walked up to her. She was trembling in fear as I walked up to her. "Your fat ass I been waiting for the opportunity." She raised her arms, "please, please, please. Don't kill me, don't kill me like you killed my brother." She looked at Danity. Danity had a shocked look on her face, "Ma?" She questioned. This bitch just could not shut up. I emptied my gun into her body. She shook as her body filled with lead. Her body hit the ground hard and heavy. I looked at Danity, "your father died of an asthma attack." I let her know. Danity nodded her head. "Let's get out of here." We walked out of the warehouse with three less problems in our life. As soon as we got in the car Danity dialed Jack. She thanked him for giving us the information we needed. We owed him that street tax that he wanted, and I told Maurice that he was going to give it to him. He wanted to be in the streets there were rules that he was going to have to follow. I was going to be with him every step of the way. Danity was on his right and Mama was on his left.

THE END!

**BE ON
THE LOOK OUT
4 THICK AS THIEVES 2**

READ THE BROKEN TRILOGY

SEE WHERE IT ALL BEGAN

Some Scars

BROKEN3

Never Heal

A Novel

New York Times Bestselling Author
Billie Dureyea Shell

PROLOGUE

Rashad I had to come up with a fucking plan to disappear quick! I had fucked up and I just did not know how I was going to tell Aniya. Man, what could I do? I thought to myself as I paced back and forth in the office of the strip club. We were doing good with our businesses and I just had to fuck everything up! She told me to quit and get out of the game, but I was being fucking hardheaded now the heat was coming down on me. I had got back in the game although I knew Mr. Richards was under investigation. Five years I started off small, no bodies, nothing! I wanted to be a kingpin but shit a nigga didn't want to get locked up behind the shit. My name wasn't ringing in the streets like I wanted it too and niggas thought I was soft. I was trying to be smart and not catch a body because the Feds would love to hang that shit over a nigga's head to testify. When Aniya seen that we were not making any dough after years of being in the game she told me to give the shit up. I agreed with her, but I just had that itch that needed to be scratched. I let this bitch Juanita make the runs for me. I was fucking her every now and then, but this bitch got caught up and snitched on me. They came for me HARD! They were quiet when they came and greeted me like a friend. They were on me every day and every night, letting me know that I was going to lose it all. When I asked them what they wanted they told me Al Richards. A nigga wasn't a snitch but what could I do. I made sure not to tell Aniya. Shit was moving fast in the investigation they had a nigga wearing a wire and everything. I felt like a hoe ass nigga every time I walked into a meeting with Mr. Richards. Two weeks ago, they finally locked up Mr. Richards and I felt a weight lift off my shoulder. Once that weight lifted a boulder came crushing down on my chest. They came to me and told me that I still needed to testify I was shook. This nigga Mr. Richards was going to kill me. He didn't know it was me who was going to testify yet, so I needed to get ghost quick. At first, I thought about telling Aniya, but I would have to explain everything. I was just not ready to do that. As I paced the floor and thought about everything my phone vibrated with a text. I looked and saw that it was Talia, my baby's mama. Talia 'I miss you.' I know I had told Aniya that her and my child were missing but I knew where they were. I would always know where Talia was at, she fucked with me through thick and thin. I had met Talia at the mall one Saturday while I was shopping. Talia was bad I mean Sanaa Lathan bad. She was gorgeous from her head to her toes. She gave me her number and told me that she was only in town with her boyfriend on some business. Yeah right you trying to throw that boyfriend shit in there I thought but you gave me the number. I wasn't even giving a fuck. She called me later that night saying her boyfriend was leaving her and she was going to be alone. I wasn't taking no chances though because shit hoes like to set up niggas especially out of town hoes. I told her to meet me at McDonalds, she did. I bought the bitch a meal and fucked her in the bathroom six weeks later she called me talking about she was pregnant. I was floored. She didn't know if it was mine or her man's baby. She kept it one hundred with the both of us and we waited for the nine months and took the test. It came back to be mine. Her nigga who they called the Reaper was pissed and kicked her out. She came to stay with me for a while but when she seen that I wasn't going to commit she up and left and moved to Jersey.

BINGO! Talia, she was it! I needed to sweet talk Talia and go to Jersey with her and my son I missed the little nigga anyways. I went to see him every other month but this time I was going to stay. I loved Aniya and I felt like she was the one and I loved her kids, but I couldn't do this shit with the Feds. I looked over at the picture that sat on my desk of me and Aniya. I picked it up and stared at her beautiful face. Damn, what was I going to do? I had never loved anybody as much as I loved her. Yes, I fucked cheap ass hoes, but no one compared to my Aniya. Damn this was going to be hard, but I had to do it. I just had to come up with the perfect plan. My phone vibrated and snapped me out of my thoughts. I had to get my shit together. Between the Feds, my damn brother, Talia, Aniya and the kids, my Mama and Daddy, and my sister Rebecca I had to get things together. I looked at my phone it was Aniya I smiled until I pulled up the text. Wifey 'So you fucking, one of those stripper hoes again! I am gone fuck around and have to kill you nigga because you playing with my emotions.' What the fuck was she talking about, I thought to myself. I was about to text her that when another text message popped up. Wifey 'why get married if you gone fuck off? You could have just left my ass in Milwaukee with the dumb shit. You used to them dumb ass country hoes I ain't the one I am from the Ill Mill nigga' Oh, shit here she go with this crazy shit. She was always talking about killing a nigga and shit. Wait, wait. That was it I had the perfect plan. Yup Jersey here I come I had to get the fuck out of Atlanta start over get me a new life. I loved my wife, but she was just a pawn in this game too fuck it.

MYA

I turned off the water and thought how great that shower felt. I had let my curly, long hair get wet while the water ran against my body. Being a mother of two children was harder than I thought. Thankfully I had my boyfriend Tre of the last five years because he was heaven sent just in the right time. The one night, Aniya and I went to a bar I had met him, and he had changed my life. His dark chocolate skin was not what I was used too, but I put my preference aside and got to know the chocolate stranger and it paid off. That night was a night to remember not only did I find the love my life, but we had also caught Niya's boyfriend at the time cheating. Hopefully he was at peace now because he was an evil man that had put my friend through hell. He was the devil reincarnated as Bruce Thompson. The man would stop at nothing to sabotage Niya, but from day one Tre had been heaven sent to me and Aniya. I thought about the time and knew I needed hurry to hurry up and get out the shower. I still had to check the books of the companies that Aniya had left in my possession and then I had to make sure I had the kids some food. Niya had left me in charge of her cleaning and home building companies. She had hired different managers. My job was to make sure the numbers looked good, that everyone was getting paid, and that all supplies was replenished at the end of the week. I did not do any of the firing and hiring but I did run background checks on the future employees and I always did pop ups. Being a spoiled brat who had nothing, but money handed to me I liked the idea of making my own money and being the boss. I could not have children, but I was a Godmother. Aniya had left me the sole guardian of her two children Malcolm and A'Deena. They were older so they pretty much could do things for themselves. Malcolm was a twelve-year old growing teenage boy and I loved that Tre had taught him certain things and always had time to spend with him. A'Deena was a ten-year old blossoming beauty that was sassy yet sweet. I adored those children but me taking care of them had been so sudden. Aniya had told me not to worry but I was worried, and I found myself stopping throughout the day to pray for my friend. Murder that was a serious crime, murder! I shook my head as I thought about it the whole thing was still unreal to me. How could my friend be on trial for murder? The last five years of Aniya's life was a complete blur to me because I had not been in Aniya's life in a while. It seemed like once Niya and Rashad got married Niya changed. She was always discreet and secretive, but she was really guarded and that scared me. Tre would always say you know she enjoying her marriage and her new family. Just think about what she has been through. Tre was always the type that looked on the brighter side and that is what I loved about him. Being a private investigator, he had seen many things but the things that we had found out about Niya's ex-boyfriend, was intolerable. I knew firsthand that Niya had been through a lot with her boyfriend Bruce. He was trying to sabotage her and take away the companies that her kid's father had left her. He was found dead in his apartment I knew Aniya was going through some kind of traumatic episode. She had married Bruce's half-brother, so something had to be going on in her head that no one was aware of. I wasn't the one to judge but damn to leave your ex-boyfriend and for his brother. I would never do that in a million years. I knew she had a thing for Rashad but to follow, through was too much. I had been supportive of her and the relationship, but it was strange to me. I tried to not think about the situation because it was too much. Matter of fact all this thinking was making my head hurt. I decided on some spaghetti and garlic bread for dinner something simple yet filling. Tre was going to be working a long shift because he was doing his job and he was also doing a side job for me. I wanted him to figure out what was going on with Niya. All my friend would say is that she is okay whenever she called which was seldom. How could she be when she was in jail facing murder charges, murder for killing her husband? This was something that I could not wrap around my head I just did not understand, and I really wanted answers. The day that Aniya had called to tell me to come get her kids it was a sunny afternoon. Tre and I had just come from a morning breakfast date. The pancakes with strawberries that we had with the whip cream had filled the spot and the sunny side eggs with the crispy bacon had me feeling sleepy. I just wanted to crawl in bed with my love and lay in his arms after that good breakfast. I had fallen in love with Tre and it felt so good. He was working so hard that he had not been around lately, but I was used to it. Plus no matter what he always came home to me. We had gone to the movies and for once our plan was to lie in the bed and just enjoy each other company at the end of the night. On the way from the movie theater my heart dropping call came in. I picked up and it was a jail call. You have a collect call from "Niya". That was all I heard, and I started panicking. I hurriedly started to accept but I did not have collect calls on my phone. I went through the prompts to put some funds on my phone. I dug through my purse and got my credit card while Tre drove and looked at me. He knew something was wrong and he wanted me to tell him. "What's wrong baby?" He asked. I had a one-track mind and was trying to register what was going on. Finally, as I punched in my credit card number, I answered him. "It's Niya she is in jail." He did not say anything because he knew that I did not know what was going on. My light face had turned to a red color and I my heart was racing as if I was the one who was locked away. After they had the money I was connected to my best friend. "Hello Niya?" It had been five years since I had taken over Niya's companies and Niya had gotten married to her husband Rashad. "Go get A'Deena and Malcolm. You know I put you as the guardian and I need you to call this number so you can go pick them up." She gave me the number. I grabbed a stick of red lipstick out of my oversized purse. I wrote the number against my light arms. I did not have a pen or paper and I did not have time to look. "What happened?" I wanted to know what was going on. "I killed Rashad." She said and my breath was taken away. Tre watched as my face lost all color. "You okay honey?" He questioned. "Wait, what?" "You heard me I am not about to repeat that shit." You could hear the annoyance in Niya's voice. "I told you if something ever happened to me to make sure you can get my kids can you do that until I get out?" She said and I shook my head yes although the only person who could see me was Tre. When I shook my head yes Tre took that as I was saying that I was okay, so he calmed down a bit. "Yes, I will get them. Do you have bail or anything?" I asked I needed to know what I needed to do and Niya was not making it easy because she wasn't telling me anything. "No just go get my kids." Niya hung up. I did not know what was going on but that was two weeks ago. Tre did not have any answers. He was using all his contacts as a private investigator but was coming up very short there was no jail records of Niya being in the jails and they had not heard anything. This was difficult and Tre said that he was going to get to the bottom of things. He was working overtime trying to get information, but none was out there. I believed in my man because he usually did so I was just patiently waiting because I was hoping that my best friend was okay. The fifteen second phone calls saying that she was okay was not enough and I needed to know more. It was strange because she was not calling from a collect number anymore so how was she calling? Tre had tried to trace the calls back to a phone line, but they were all throw away phones. If she had throwaway phones, then where was she at? All these unanswered questions that I needed to know because I wanted to tell her kids something. That was another strange thing the kids had not really said anything about what was going on. When I would ask them, they would just say my Mama is coming back to get us that is all she told us. As I slipped on my clothes I had so many questions whirling through my head. I just needed to occupy my mind by cooking. As I stood in the kitchen stirring the noodles the question just kept coming to mind. If she knows that she is coming back to get them what is really going on?

Chapter Two
MYA

Niya and I had met in Middle School. I was always a quiet girl and so was Niya. Niya was always a pretty girl and I could never understand why she really did not talk to anyone. Niya always had short hair that was always kept up in a cute style. I on the other hand always had that curly long hair that I was proud to have. I did not talk to the kids in the school because they liked to keep up drama and gossip. My father had told me that the last thing a girl should be caught up in is some bullshit. All kids our age liked to do was talk bad about each other and to be honest none of them were anything special. All the girls dressed the same and wore their hair the same. All the boys wore the same clothes and tried to keep up with the latest shoes nothing was unique about any of them. I did not understand why they talked about each other. The day that Niya and I became friends was the worst day of my young teenage life. I came to school to find out this guy that I had a crush on made up a rumor about me giving him head. I had never put my lips on or near a boy's private area and for him to lie about that was really embarrassing to me. I had been quiet and had not said anything to anyone. I noticed the stares, but I just kept quiet. His girlfriend on the other hand was ready to fight her name was Sharita. Sharita did not like the idea of some other chick trying to get with her man. She had never seen me talking to her boyfriend, but she just went along with the rumor. Sure, I had flirted with the guy, but I never made a move on him. Sharita was a big booty brown skinned beauty that loved drama. Niya had heard all the talk about how Sharita and her three friends Raquel, Starla, and Nicole were going to jump me. It was lunch time and the girls surrounded me and started cursing me out. "Bitch your little prissy ass going to get your ass beat today." Sharita said with her stinky ass breath. "I don't want to fight you." I said in a calm tone I was scared because I did want to get jump and they mess up my pretty face. "Bitch you not going to fight me I am going to beat your ass." Sharita shot back and the crowd started laughing. "Whatever," I said and tried to walk away and that is when Sharita pushed me. She wasn't prepared for the lock that met her face. I had put a lock in a sock courtesy of my Mother who told me even if I got jumped to give them hell. I started swinging my hands and I clocked Sharita upside her head. It stunned her but Raquel came back on me and hit me in my head, and it dazed me. That gave the other girls the fuel to jump in the fight. They really didn't know how to fight, and I was giving as good as I was getting. Sharita screamed "Bitch want to fuck my man!" That is when Niya jumped into help me. She could not believe these girls were fighting me over a boy. Niya started punching the girls and since they were not aware that anyone was going to help me, they were not prepared for the blows. We all got suspended that day and Niya and I became best friends. I was beaten up a bit and had bruises on my face, but I was okay it could have been worse had Niya not jumped in. After that we were inseparable. Niya had met my father who was white and my mother who was black. I had met her mother and she was beautiful. I did not know if she was mixed like me because whenever I asked Niya where her father was, she would say gone. If I kept pushing the question, she would get upset. I told my Mama about it and she broke it down to me. She told me that Niya probably did not know where her father was and that I needed to stop asking her, so I did. Niya would let me come spend the night with her when her mother would leave her on the weekends. I would sometimes ask Niya where was her mother. Niya would make up an excuse and say that her mother worked third shift. Although we were best friends Niya never told me anything about what she was going through. I was the one who talked. I talked to Niya about all my problems and she gave good advice but when ever I asked Niya if she had any problems then she would just act as if everything was okay. I had been trying to figure out how I was going to ever get in touch with Niya when I checked the mail and all my questions were answered. There was a letter addressed to me but there was not a return address. I was skeptical of looking at the letter for that very reason. It was late and Tre had not come home yet. I had put the kids in their room. It was better that the kids were older because they pretty much took care of themselves because I had never taken care of babies although I loved children. I cleaned up the kitchen and tried to watch television until Tre got home. My mind was restless and after a while I could no longer take it and I opened the letter and was surprised to see that it was from Niya. Dear Mya, Hey boo I know you worried about me but trust and believe that I am good. I hope my kids are being good I miss them so much. I remember the first time I found out I was pregnant by Hakeem it was the happiest day of my life which turned into my worst nightmare. No lie I loved the man to death, but he was an evil man. I know I am not the talkative type and I am not open. I have to let you know you are my best friend and every time I need you, you are always there. You are special to me because you never question me. You just do it and you are so sincere. Anyways I just wanted you to know that I am doing good and I am okay. I know Tre is trying to find me, but he will not be able to find me because it is much deeper than you may know. Once everything is over, I will tell you everything but right now is not the best time to tell you because I do not know who is watching. Kiss my kids for me and keep them safe I know you will keep them safe. Love you Niya That was the letter that was it and that was all. She did not leave a return address or tell me about her case. I was starting to doubt that Niya was in jail since we had not found her yet. This was so strange. Niya called that first day and she called to make sure I had her kids. After that the calls were just a few seconds letting me know that she was okay. I did not know what she was saying about Hakeem I thought he was a pretty okay guy. Niya was a woman with many secrets though. She did tell me that he used hit her though, maybe that is what she meant. We had not seen each other since Niya's honeymoon. I would try to connect with her but Niya was always too busy.

She had left me in control of her companies, and I would deposit her money right into her account that was her portion. Niya had other businesses that she was into. I did not know what they were because I had my hands full with the ones, she had left me in charge of. I did not know that being a businesswoman could be so hard thankfully I was born into the business. I had gotten advice from my father who owned hotels across the county. My big sister Monica also was a businesswoman in Michigan. Other than Niya, Monica was my best friend who I talked about everything with. I had told my sister certain things about Niya but I really did not have anything to go off of. Monica had been telling me for years that girl is dangerous. I didn't know how true that was. All the years we had known each other, and I knew so little about my friend. I felt special because she felt safe enough to leave her kid's in my custody, so I knew that Niya loved and respected me, but she was just so private. It also made me wonder with Niya being so private what else was she hiding though. To just up and call me and break some news to me about killing Rashad that was just crazy. The chills ran up my spine to even think that Niya could be capable of something like murder. My father was another special part of my life he made it so that we would be well taken care of. Before I started working for Niya I was just a receptionist and although I liked my job to be the boss was something new to me. Yes, I could have helped my father with his business, but I wanted to branch off and do my own thing and I was happy that Niya had trusted me so much. I did not know what that letter meant but I was going to show Tre. I went to the other bedroom where Malcolm and Deena slept. They had to share rooms because Tre and I only had a two-bedroom home. I saw that they were still awake, and I went to tell them that I had contact with their mother. Even if it was just a letter something was better than nothing. "Malcolm, Deena I got a letter from your Mom." I had not really asked them about the events that took place because I did not know what to say. I did not know if they saw their Mom kill their stepfather or what. "She doing okay?" Malcolm asked. I felt bad for the kids. They had lost their father and now they may lose their mother. "Yes, she fine honey she did not tell me much about what was going on, but she did say she was okay." "Oh, I know what is going on. I just wanted to make sure she was okay." He said. I looked at him in surprise. "Well what is going on?" I wanted to know. Malcolm looked up at the wall. He was becoming quite a handsome young man. He looked a lot like his father. "A lot but Mama said she would explain everything to you." That is what he said but I could tell it was something else to what he was saying but

I could not read between the lines. I needed to talk to Tre. That night Tre made it home around two and he woke me up when he got in the bed. I was restless anyway, so it was easy for him to stir me. He put his arms around my waist, and I turned towards him. I kissed his nose and he smiled. "Baby Niya wrote me a letter but she did not leave a return address." "What you mean?" He asked getting excited. "She did not leave a return address." I repeated it again. Tre jumped up. "Let me see the letter." Although Tre was exhausted, he jumped back on to the scene like he was at work. He got up early at six in the morning and went to work every morning. People would think that I would be tripping not to see my man all day and half of the night, but I understood he was out making money. I got up and went to the drawer and pulled the letter out. I handed it to Tre, and he looked at the envelope. It was a regular envelope and it looked normal, but he noticed one thing that I had not noticed. "Babe where did you get this letter?" "The mailbox what you mean she mailed it to me you see it's in an envelope." "How when there is no stamp on the envelope" He said and showed me the envelope...........

Tre Mya was acting stupid as hell. I know damn well she knew this envelope did not have a damn stamp on it. Her pretty ass just sitting here with her hair all wild and looking at me like I was crazy. One thing I loved about Mya was that she was naïve. It was cute and I adored her. I had been dating her for five years and I had fallen in love with this woman. I know a man like me is not supposed to fall in love, but I had and as much as I hated to lie to her I did it every single day. I told Mya that I am a private investigator and that is true for the most part but when I find my, target I kill them. I am a hired hitman and I am good at my job. I am one of the most top paid hitmen. It hurts me to pretend to be broke for Mya. The truth is it also makes me feel good that she is not dating me for my money but because she actually loves me. To be honest I love everything about the woman. That crazy ass wild hair of hers, the fact that she doesn't nag me, the way she keeps my food warm no matter how late I come home. She loves me and I love her but this friend of hers, Aniya she is all trouble. Ever since I met Mya, Aniya has had problem after problem. I know everything even though she does not know I know. I know about the suspicious death of her baby daddy Hakeem. Bruce, I have my own suspicions just because they were having so many problems and then BAM the nigga is dead. Plus, I know that her husband Rashad ain't shit. She thinks he is hot shit, but that nigga is dangerous. I don't know what it is about Aniya but from one killer to the next I know that she is a killer. She hides it well and she is remarkable at killing without a trace. Now this bitch has disappeared, and I can't even find her. I have everybody on this shit, and we cannot find her that can only mean one thing she is working with the Feds. In that case I can't even touch that. I do my dirty work with the local police I ain't that stupid to get twisted with the Feds. I could see the worry on my lady's face, and I wanted to make it right. I grabbed Mya and held her. She pushed away from me. I knew what that meant she was worried so that meant I had to really come up with some way to get her distracted, but I just did not know how. From day one I had been there trying to win Mya's heart. I think I did that when I kept helping her out with Aniya's problems. These five years with her moving to Atlanta was the best. I knew her husband was selling drugs for some Mexican Al Richards. I did not know everything that was going on, but I knew that much. I was happy that Aniya had left us alone. Mya wanted to know why her friend had changed on her. I told her that she was enjoying her marriage and to leave it like that. Honestly, I was happy though she was too many problems. Now here she was five years later causing more problems and once again we had her kids.

Chapter Three

MYA

I had tossed and turned that entire night. I still did not have any answers for what I had learned. How the hell can an envelope be mailed without a stamp? It couldn't so that meant that someone dropped it off to me but whom? I had not heard anyone in the driveway, and I did not hear a car so who could have delivered it? Niya was supposed to be in jail so who could deliver it? This had my head all messed up. All day I tried to busy myself with work, but I was dragging and not focused at all. My mind kept going back to the letter and I wanted answers I felt that I was owed that much. I called Tre at work to see if he could give me some answers. He still did not know what was going on and he had taken the letter to work with him. I decided to get my mind off the mystery because truth be told I could not do anything about it. I asked Deena if she wanted to come with me and go to the nail shop. Malcolm said he wanted to stay behind so I told him that it would be okay. He was old enough and he was going to stay in the house. Deena and I had a great time. I really did enjoy spending time with my Goddaughter especially since I could not have any kids of my own. It hurt when I thought about it, but I knew that it was meant to be. Everyone did not need a child sometimes that was not what life had in store for them. I knew that one day I would be blessed with the life that I wanted and needed. I knew that it was near. After years of dealing with Chris's bullshit and his baby mama drama I was happy that I was free to do as I pleased. Tre was everything I was looking for. Sometimes I was upset because he worked long hours, but he always came home to me one thing Chris never had done. Chris at first was a sweet guy we had been dating since High School. He was a tall blonde white guy and he was awesome just as much as he was handsome. He was a fun guy to be around and when I found that the popular guy in school was into me it made my heart flutter. I could still feel the way my stomach fluttered when Niya came up to me and told me that Chris liked me. I had just finished my fifth period class and was waiting for Niya to come to our lockers that we shared so that we could enjoy lunch together. I had my hair in a cute bun on top of my head. My sister Monica had flattened my hair and my long, curly hair had transformed into some long, straight hair that went to my butt. Niya came up to me with a scrunched face that looked like she was annoyed. Niya had gotten bigger since Middle School. All the guys looked at her butt and talked about how big her butt was. I thought my friend was coming to tell me about another perverted guy. "Girl guess who like you?" In an aggravated tone. "Who?" I asked feeling excited since we had started High School two years ago. I had not had a boyfriend. Niya had one boyfriend who she kept saying was not her boyfriend, but they were always with each other. "Chris ugh" Niya rolled her eyes to show her hatred for him. "Really?" I had a secret crush on the guy who Niya did not like. Niya said that Chris was a jerk, but she didn't even know him. "Ugh girl you like him too" Niya said laughing and I smiled. "I guess I will give him your number since you crushing on his big head ass too." After that everything was history from there Niya eventually started liking Chris because at first, he treated me so sweet. After High School we made our life together well we were supposed to. So, when he started cheating it was so confusing and it hurt me something awful. Everytime I called Niya she was there to hear my problems. Niya never judged she just listened. Niya did not like Chris after she heard that he cheated on me, but she never told me I should leave. It was my decision Niya was just there to listen. That was what a best friend was supposed to do not judge but listen. So now that Aniya was having problems I was there to listen and to help in any way. A favor for a favor. Niya never talked about anything that she was going through in her life. I actually loved the last couple of months before she got married because Niya was very open and I got to see my friend in action. Niya was so smart, sassy, and in a way conniving. Although we all make mistakes in life it was like Niya would crisscross through every obstacle and zigzag into her destiny. She was strong and I loved that about her. When she got married and became distant, I just did not understand. I had hoped everything was okay and although we had the casual conversations about the business and money, we never talked like we had before I truly missed my best friend. When I got the call that Niya was in jail it scared me because I really was worried about my friend. When Deena and I made it back to the house I called out to Malcolm. I had bought some Popeye's Chicken on the way from the salon and I was starving. Deena had been quiet most of the time when we were gone. I was trying to get some information out of the little girl but the harder I tried the quieter she got. I told Deena to go upstairs and get her brother. "Malcolm not upstairs"

Deena came back downstairs and said to me. I was confused. "What you mean he not upstairs?" I asked as I pulled the chicken out of the bag. "He not up there he gone." Deena said and I dropped the coleslaw on the floor and ran up the stairs. I screamed out Malcolm's name and didn't get an answer. I ran to his room and he was not in there. I ran to the bathroom and he was not in there. I was sweating and panicking, and my curly hair was all over my head. I called Tre and he didn't answer I didn't know what to do. I went back into the room that the kids shared and sat on the bed that belonged to Malcolm. I sat in total shock, where was he? There was no trace of any one being in the house. I could not believe that the boy was gone. I should have never left him alone. I did not know what was going on, but I ran downstairs to make sure Deena was there. Deena was sitting at the table eating her food. "Did you find Malcolm?" She asked through bites. I looked at her beautiful face with her curly long hair she kind of reminded me of me when I was little. "Yeah he okay honey." "Mama must have came to get him while we were gone." I just looked at the little girl. I did not know what to say I did not know how to tell her that her brother was taken, and it was my fault for leaving him alone. I plopped down next to Deena, but I did not eat. I was too worried. I wish I had not gotten my nails done because I wanted to bite on them nails so bad. After Deena got finished eating, we went into the living room to watch television. My mind was not there. As she laughed at Patrick and Spongebob, I sat there crying inside I had fucked up. Tre still had not called me back and I did not know if I should call the police or what I should do. I was just going to sit and wait to see what was going on because I was scared and puzzled. The butterflies in my stomach were not helping and I felt as if I was going to be sick. Niya had trusted me with her most precious gifts and I had been stupid enough to let them out of my sight. I felt that Malcolm was old enough to watch himself but what I didn't know was that someone was watching him. This upset me that someone could come in my house where I was supposed to feel safe and take him out of there. And why the fuck had Tre not called me back? Did they not know that my fiancée was a private investigator who worked for the police? Obviously, whoever it was didn't care. I had fallen asleep in the room with Deena because I was scared that Deena would come up missing too. I felt Tre tugging at me in the middle of the night. Tired and baffled I walked into the room with him. "Where Malcolm at?" He asked pulling off his work shirt. "I don't know." I was still a bit sleep. "What you mean you don't know?" He walked up to me and gave me a kiss. "Somebody took him" I cried as it hit me all at once I had lost Malcolm it was too much for me. "What you mean somebody took him? Took him from where?" Tre voice had gotten loud. "I called you and you did not answer, and you did not call me back. When Deena and I went to the nail shop… when we came back, he was gone." I cried I was now fully awake. "Why didn't you call the police or anything. I would have gotten that call." Tre screamed and walked towards his shirt. "I was waiting for you to call me back!" I screamed. "Bullshit Mya! You know what is going on here you better tell me more because this shit don't make sense. You call me for everything else and you won't call me for something serious like your best friend son coming up missing? What the fuck that don't sound right! How did the person get in?" Tre screamed you could tell that he was noticeably angry. He had never yelled at me and he had never had a reason too. "Are you trying to say that I had something to do with this? You fucking asshole he's my Godson! I don't know how they got in." I stormed out the room and went back to sleep in the kids' room. I was upset and I did not know how Tre could accuse me of making my own Godson disappear. I sat and thought about it for a minute. No, I did not call the police when I should have but I was scared because I really did not know what to do. All this mysterious bullshit was new to me. All this was new to me I had grown up sheltered and loved. I did not know what to do with missing children and best friends being in jail. I started crying again I could not believe I had let this happen. I heard Tre come into the room. He was by the doorway. "I am sorry okay. I just don't understand why you wouldn't think this is urgent? You have to think Mya this shit is serious." I knew that I wasn't a kid. "It's bad already that no one can find Niya and every time I call the Atlanta Police department, I am not getting any information. You say she is in jail? But no one can find her. You need to think really hard because we need answers because now her son is missing, and they want to know where she is. Who can help us out?" Huh he was getting on my nerves hell he was the damn investigator. I had not been close to Niya in five years. Out of the blue she calls me and tells me that she killed her husband and that I need to get my God kids. I did not know what the hell was going on, but everything was getting on my nerves already. I did not know what to do or how to handle this situation. I was used to a quiet lifestyle except for the dumb relationships I had ended up in. But Tre was right I was in the middle of it so it was time to think. Who could we call to see what might have happened? Who did I know that Niya knew? Damn no one. Niya's mother was dead, she didn't know her father, and Rashad's brother was dead oh wait. "Rebeccca!" I screamed. We had gone to Chicago and met Bruce and Rashad's sister Rebecca before. "Yeah pack your shit we going to Chicago." Tre said.

Tre I really needed to find this bitch Niya and quick. She was turning my world upside down. I had been looking for her everywhere. I mean I didn't know the chick like that, but I know she was my woman's best friend. Mya was not letting me touch her ever since them kids moved in. From day one I treated Malcolm and Deena like my own they were easy to love. Malcolm was smart. One day he may be a trained killer if he stuck around me. Deena she was quiet a princess. She was the type of girl that you just wanted to protect. Those beautiful hazel eyes just made her much more innocent. I wanted to find their mother to help these kids. I was a killer no lie, but I had a heart. Everything about me was not just kill, kill, kill. I loved Mya she was the closest thing I had to family and her family accept me. I loved every bit of it. Her sister Monica was sweet, Monica's husband Joey was a real cool dude too, straight square. I didn't have anyone but my brother Ken. He was all that I had left. He was everything to me. Niya had even hired him as a manager for her companies. I loved that so I was going to take the extra time to find her. Once Malcolm disappeared,

I got worried. I didn't mean to snap at Mya, but she was acting stupid as hell. Like come on this shit is serious and you didn't think to call me. I need for her to have her head on straight. This shit is serious. Then on top of that someone broke into our home and took Malcolm. Niggas knew who I was in this area, so I knew it wasn't a person from here. They left no trace too. I mean they went in and out in no time. I even checked the locks there were little scratch marks, but the lock was not damaged whoever this guy was he was good. I was happy that Mya had finally used that pretty head of hers for not just looking cute and to actually think. Rebecca, I knew for a fact that she was married to Rashad's brother on his mother's side Darien. She might be the key to everything. I thought that it was sick for them to be married but whatever floats their boats. Rebecca had told us a sick ass story about their brother Bruce. I know Aniya felt stupid as hell she was sleeping with that white boy and he was foul. I was laughing inside at her ass. I loved Mya but Aniya was fine as hell. She needed her a nigga that white boy didn't know what to do with all those curves. Mya is skinny and fit while Aniya got a fat ass. I mean you can't help but too look. When I met Mya, I was checking out the both of them really. So, when she Mya gave me the go ahead, I went for her. It was just something about the way she looked so innocent and pure. She had to be mine. I was happy that she was the one who came to talk to me. The way bodies were dropping around Aniya I might had been next. Mya was the perfect one for me. As soon as I figure all this shit out, I am going to marry that woman.

ABOUT
THE AUTHOR

New York Times & International Best Selling Author
Billie Dureyea Shell was born in Compton California and
now lives in Ladera Heights with his wife and
kids who he loves to spend time with.

He is the Owner of several properties in the Los Angeles
area and gives back to his community by providing low
income housing to those who need it.

He stated "It doesn't matter where you at or where you
from it's what you do with your time. There's nothing you
can't do if you put your mind to it".